The Woman on the Train

Rupert Colley

Rupert Colley

Rupert Colley was born one Christmas Day and grew up in Devon. A history graduate, he worked as a librarian in London before starting 'History In An Hour' – a series of non-fiction history ebooks that can be read in just sixty minutes, acquired by Harper Collins in 2011. Now a full time writer, he lives in Waltham Forest, London with his wife, two children and dog.

Fiction:
The Woman on the Train
The White Venus
The Black Maria
My Brother the Enemy
Anastasia
This Time Tomorrow
The Unforgiving Sea
The Red Oak

History In An Hour series:
1914: History In An Hour
Black History: History In An Hour
D-Day: History In An Hour
Hitler: History In An Hour
Mussolini: History In An Hour
Nazi Germany: History In An Hour
Stalin: History **In** An Hour
The Afghan Wars: History In An Hour
The Cold War: History In An Hour
The Russian Revolution: History In An Hour
The Siege of Leningrad: History In An Hour
World War One: History In An Hour
World War Two: History In An Hour

Other non-fiction:
The Savage Years: Tales From the 20th Century
The Hungarian Revolution, 1956
The Battle of the Somme
A History of the World Cup: An Introduction

The Woman on the Train

Rupertcolley.com

Part One

Annecy, September 1982

I was expecting a visitor. The first, perhaps, in years. I can't remember. The prospect had put me on edge for days. And today was the day. He was due at one o'clock. I had a shave, and took an age deciding whether I should wear a tie and, if so, what colour. Not too bright or garish, not too sombre. In the end, I plumped for a muted green. I had a tidy up in recognition of this momentous occasion – threw away newspapers that should have been thrown away weeks, if not months, ago, cleaned the toilet, pushed the vacuum cleaner around, plumped the cushions, rearranged them several times. I dusted the pictures on the wall, especially the framed newspaper cuttings featuring me back in the days when I was *something*.

Then, with nothing else to occupy myself with, I sat down on the edge of my settee, hands neatly on my lap, and waited, checking my watch. One o'clock came and went. At five minutes past one, the doorbell rang. He was five minutes late. Not that I blamed him — trying to find this address in this backwater French provincial town near the Swiss border is no mean feat. And he'd come some distance — over 500 kilometres, all the way from Paris.

He'd phoned me a few days earlier. His name was Henri Bowen, a Frenchman with an Englishman's name, a journalist from one of the nationals, I forget which now. He'd said he was writing an article about people who'd made a name for themselves during the sixties but had since faded from public view. A sort of 'where are they now?'-type piece. I had hesitated and told him I would consider it and ring him back. And I did think about it — in fact, I thought of nothing else all day. I was tempted, of course; it appealed to my vanity, a trait I thought I'd repressed years ago. Obviously not. For I was once a very vain man. But I was comfortable with that — to be a leading light in one's chosen profession, a degree of vanity is a necessity. But since my downfall, no, let's call it retirement, many years ago, I'd been content to fade into obscurity. Did I want to be remembered? Of course I did. The chance may never present itself again. The following day, I phoned up this Monsieur Bowen and, as I knew I would, told him yes, I'd be happy to be interviewed. He seemed delighted.

And here he is, sitting in my ever-so tidy living room, the place smelling of air freshener. Good-looking fellow, slicked-back hair, positively shiny, tall, very pale, wearing a dapper cream-coloured suit, firm handgrip. 'It's lovely to meet you, Maestro.'

'Oh please, Monsieur Bowen, less of the maestro. I'm a plain old Monsieur now, and happy to be so.'

He refused my offer of tea and biscuits, and, at my invitation, sat down on my settee which sucked him in, leaving him looking slightly awkward. He took in his surroundings and, I have to confess, despite my efforts at cleaning up, I felt a prick of shame. There was no denying it – I lived in such a mundane place. The chintzy carpets, the turquoise curtains, the squashy settee, the old-fashioned radio – nothing wrong with any of it but it must have seemed very ordinary to a thrusting young man like Henri Bowen. Given my former fame, given the respect I used to command, he must have expected a lot more. I could see the words written all over his face – 'how the mighty have fallen'. He tried his best to cover up his embarrassment. 'My parents had all your records,' he said, almost falling over his words. 'They loved everything you did. I think the Richard Strauss was their favourite.'

I sat down opposite him, crossing my legs. 'Your parents had fine tastes, Monsieur Bowen.'

He laughed politely. 'As far as they were concerned, if it had your name on it then it had to be good.' So, what happened? He didn't say it – but from the expression on his face, he might as well have done. 'Do you have any of your own records?'

'No.' His reaction obliged me to explain. 'One's musical direction changes all the time. What I felt was right twenty years ago, now makes me... how shall I say... cringe. With age, I look back at my cavalier approach, and at the liberties I took, and I feel, well, if not embarrassed, then certainly a little bashful. I fear my younger self had a rather inflated opinion of himself, thinking he knew better than the composers he was trying to interpret.'

'Do you listen to much music now?'

'No, not often. I prefer Moroccan music nowadays.'

'That surprises me. Do you mind if I take notes?'

'Be my guest. Tell me, Monsieur Bowen, I don't mind, but how long do you think this'll take? It's just that everyday at three, I like to pop over and visit an elderly neighbour. I like to make sure they're OK.'

'Plenty of time.'

'I don't need to visit, really, but I feel as if I'm doing my bit.'

As he organised himself with pad and pen, rummaging in

his briefcase, he mentioned a photographer. 'It'd only take a few minutes,' he said. 'She's very good. Based locally. I'll get her to give you a call.'

'I used to have my photo taken several times a day. This will be the first for many a year.' I wasn't sure how I felt about it. Part of me was, for sure, thrilled, but the idea of the whole country seeing me, as I am now, a shadow of my former self, perturbed me.

'You look different from the photos.'

'We all get older, Monsieur Bowen.'

'No, it's not that – it's something about your nose, I think. Sorry, that sounds rude.'

'It's a long story.'

'Would you mind if I smoked?'

'I would.'

He took this little setback in his stride. 'I've done my research and read about you in the papers and mags. You did a lot of interviews back then.'

'I was a man in demand, Monsieur Bowen.'

'Yes,' he said with a flicker of a smile. 'I know, before your success as a conductor, you were a hero of the resistance.'

'A hero? I may have exaggerated a little.' I'd often had that, *Hero of the Resistance*. The label always made me squirm uncomfortably. Drumming my fingers on my knee, I tried to explain. 'The words resistance and hero are too often merged together, as if by merely being in the resistance automatically made you a hero. Yes, I was in the resistance, as you know, but I never did anything remotely heroic.' Bowen tried to speak. I cut him short with my hand in the air. 'Yes, if I had been caught it would have been unpleasant but I was, how do you say these days, small fry. I was not on any list; I knew nothing. Occasionally, I'd be given an errand which might have carried an element of risk but that was about it. I would do my task, without fuss, and go home again.'

'Yes, I read about what you said. Nonetheless, back then, during the war, they must have been difficult times.'

'Oh yes, I can't deny that. One had no control over one's life. I'd always wanted to conduct. Before the war, I had secured myself a place at a music college but the Germans invaded before I had chance to take up my place. After that... well.' I waved my hands in the air. He understood. 'Instead I was forced into conducting invisible orchestras on my father's gramophone player playing Vivaldi or Elgar, or whatever was that week's favourite. Before the war, we listened, as a family, to concerts on the radio but once the Germans took over, radios were banned.'

'In case you listened to the BBC, or something like that.'

'Precisely that. We had to hand our radios in. That was a

sad day for me. But, really, Monsieur Bowen, about my war years, I have nothing to say that could be of interest to you. Except perhaps…'

He sat forward, his pen poised over his pad. 'Go on.'

'I met a woman once.' He raised an eyebrow, a sort of man-to-man acknowledgement. 'No, no, nothing like that.' I laughed inwardly. If only it had been that simple, I thought. But no, this woman was to have a far greater impact on my life than any wife or mistress could ever have had.

'Ah yes, the woman on the train. Of course, this is what our readers want to know — how you feel about it now, all these years later.'

I feared as much. Decades of hard work and creative endeavour, undone in an instant. My heartbeat quickened. I spoke, keeping my voice even, reciting words I'd rehearsed because it always came back to this. 'It's strange, isn't it, how an innocuous meeting can have such repercussions, in this instance, many, many years down the line. She was much older than me for one thing. It was the summer of forty-two. I was just twenty years old. Still a boy really, although at the time I thought of myself as a man.' I paused.

'Are you OK, Monsieur?'

'Yes. Just give me a moment.'

He leant back in the settee and gazed round the room,

pretending to show an interest in the newspaper cuttings and landscape paintings I have framed on the walls. Obscure paintings of no value by forgotten artists. Placing my fingertips against my temples, I tried to think. Did I really want to share this story with, in effect, the huge readership of a national newspaper? I had lost everything, pride was all that remained, and now I seemed on the verge of losing that too. I knew that for many people of my generation I was one of those 'Whatever happened to…' personalities. Was it not better for it to remain that way; to allow my former achievements to speak for themselves? I would regret it, I knew I would, but that vain streak was too strong to resist. I had had my years in the limelight followed by many more in obscurity. I thought I was old enough, mature enough, not to be tempted by the lure of fame any more. Could I resist one last passing shot at being at the centre of attention, at being the name on people's lips? No, sadly I couldn't; this was my one last grab at the chalice of infamy.

'Monsieur Bowen?'

'Maestro?' He sat up, struggling against the suction of the settee, trying unsuccessfully to hide his enthusiasm.

'You're right, somehow my whole life has been influenced by, as you call her, the woman on the train…'

Part Two

Saint-Romain, August 1942

I'd bought my train ticket, a return, and waited at the far end of the platform, pacing up and down, my satchel under my arm. It was almost midday on a cool and dull summer's day, heavy clouds dominating the sky. But I was hot, conscious of the dark patches of sweat under my jacket. I just needed to get this over and done with, so I could go home and hunker down. Above me, a large hanging sign with the word *Sortie*, 'Exit'. The train was due any moment. Patting my pockets, I checked for the umpteenth time for my identity card and the paper permitting my travel – I was visiting my old piano teacher, and that was the story I had to keep to. I was indeed visiting a former piano teacher in Saint-Romain, so if checked, my story would hold. Nonetheless, my stomach flitted with butterflies. Nearby, a couple of mothers with pushchairs shared a cigarette, passing it from one to the other, while talking animatedly. One of the children played with a knitted tiger, his

13

eyes crossed in concentration. Further along, also waiting, was a group of German soldiers. The sight of their uniforms always made me shudder, today especially so. They seemed in a jovial mood, as if they were a group of sightseers out on a day trip. Perhaps they were. They seemed so young, no older than me. I knew if my nation hadn't been defeated so quickly I would have been forced to join up by now, I'd be in uniform and handed a rifle and expected to fight. Craning my neck, I spied a couple of older soldiers, further along, who seemed to view their younger colleagues with a degree of exasperation. It seemed strange to think that, unbeknownst to them, I was working with the local resistance, doing tasks, albeit minor ones, that would help undermine their authority. I hated it, having too nervous a disposition for such gallant deeds, but when I was asked, what could I do? I could hardly say no and risk being labelled a collaborator. My contact, the man who, somehow, against my better judgement, recruited me was a flat-nosed tough called Gapon. Monsieur Gapon. I feared Gapon and the hard men of the resistance more than I feared the Germans. But this was how life was. One had to choose, to take sides. A young man like me was not allowed the luxury of neutrality. This was the second time Gapon had sent me on such a mission — to take information written on a sheet of paper and deliver it to fellow resisters in the town of Saint-

14

Romain, a train ride of less than half an hour. I needed to think of an excuse to avoid any further missions. The man I'd replaced, a twenty-year-old, like me, had been caught. The Gestapo had tortured him horribly. He was too weak to withstand them, and, as a result, many more were arrested. His name was mud now; he'd betrayed his fellow countrymen. But I sympathised because I knew, if caught, I'd be squealing names out before they'd even touched me. Not that it would do the Gestapo much good. The names were all codenames. Anyway, once they'd finished with the poor man, they sent him to Germany to work in a labour camp. A death sentence in all but name.

I heard the vibration of the train track and, moments later, could see the train approaching, a huge, ugly thing with its fender protruding from the front. I didn't have to worry about having to share a carriage with the Boche – they always had their own carriages, the first class ones, reserved for their exclusive use. The station guard appeared, a busy-looking fellow with his green flag tucked under his arm. The train puffed large clouds of black smoke into the clouds. A couple of men jumped off before the train had fully come to a stop and embraced the two young mothers. The little boy dropped his tiger. I called out. His mother saw, picked it up, and thanked me. I felt stupidly grateful for her kind words. I boarded the last carriage as, further up, the soldiers pushed and jostled each other like a bunch of overexcited kids. I found a near-empty compartment. Sliding the door open, I asked its sole occupant, an older woman sitting by the window, if I could join her. She waved her hand by means of saying yes, fine, whatever. I sat in the middle of the row of seats, not wanting to sit directly opposite her. No one joined us and after a few minutes, the guard outside blew his whistle and the train pulled out of the station.

Soon, we were out in the open countryside. I twirled my thumbs, crossed and uncrossed my legs, feeling sick to the core, knowing I was carrying information that could land me in front of the Gestapo. The compartment smelt slightly of the woman's perfume. I stared out at the passing countryside, seeing farmers in their fields, a horse pulling a plough, pass a village centred round a church, its spire attracting the eye. After a few minutes, I opened my satchel and retrieved my reading material – the sheet music to Wagner's opera, *Tristan and Isolde*. I didn't feel like reading but I was told to – it'd make me look more *normal*. So, I thought, if I had to read, it might as well be music. I wasn't a big fan of Wagner, far too Teutonic and self-important for my liking, but my man in the village had persuaded me that, if questioned, it'd look better to be reading something German than French.

16

I was tempted to sneak a look at the contents of the illicit envelope Monsieur Gapon had handed me, the one causing me such anxiety, now nestled in my satchel. I had no idea of its contents. But I knew it was better that way. All I knew was that I had to deliver it to a woman who worked at the station at Saint-Romain. I wouldn't miss her, Gapon told me – she was African. I puffed my cheeks – this was awful; this was not my calling. I'd been placed here on this earth to conduct music. My time, I knew, would come. The war had hindered my grand plans, but it couldn't last forever, and when, finally, men braver than me had driven the Germans off our land and defeated them, then I'd be ready.

I'd not gotten far in the score, no more than the end of the opening scene, when I considered the woman opposite. She had her eyes closed, her hands on her lap, a large handbag, more like a briefcase, at her feet. She wasn't as old as I had originally thought – middle aged, in her fifties, perhaps, nicely dressed with a burgundy-coloured jacket with heavy black stitching and a large-collared white blouse. Her skin looked tough, as if many layers deep, yet surprisingly smooth. She had jet-black hair swept up in a bun, with matching, prominent eyebrows. She had a solid-looking nose, deep-set eyes and a prominent forehead, and downturned lips. She reminded me of a bad-tempered schoolmistress. She opened her eyes, taking me by surprise, and looked straight at me – as if aware I'd been scrutinising her. I tried to turn away but too late. I felt her eyes bore into me; this time it was her turn to consider me. When I stole a glance at her, she was still staring straight at me, unblinking, with a distinct look of disapproval. Unnerved, I returned my attention to the Wagner and pretended to read.

'What is that you're studying?' Her voice confirmed the image of the old schoolmistress – loud, sharp and well-articulated, like someone in a hurry.

'I, er, it's Wagner,' I stuttered, unable to meet her eyes.

She didn't answer for a few moments, as if considering this morsel of information. Eventually, she asked. 'Why not a French composer?'

Oh, the irony, I thought. 'I study them as well. Debussy, Ravel, Bizet—'

'You don't have to list them, I am perfectly aware of who they are.'

'Yes. Sorry.'

'There's no need to apologise,' she said. 'You study music?'

'Not at the moment but one day I will be a conductor.'

'Oh, you will, will you? You sound very sure of yourself.'

This time, I looked at her directly as I said firmly, 'Yes. A conductor.'

Finally, she took her eyes off me. 'I wish you the very best of luck,' she said, looking outside the window at a passing woodland.

I returned my attention to the score but although she seemed, thankfully, to have lost interest in me, I could no longer concentrate. For some reason, our short conversation had unsettled me.

I looked at my watch – we'd be there in less than a quarter of an hour.

A few minutes later, the compartment door opened abruptly. My heart jumped. Standing at the doorway, deeply intimidating, were two German soldiers. 'Papers,' barked the first one, a tall man with small, steely-blue eyes, wearing a peaked cap, and a swastika on an armband. I'd been in this situation before and got away with it. This was worse – my exchange with the woman had made me nervous. I knew it was obvious but I lacked the strength to control my trembling hands. While I fumbled in my pockets for my card and papers, the woman passed her documents to the German. He glanced at them and with a nod of the head returned them to her. '*Dankeschön*,' she said, putting them back in her inside pocket.

'And you,' he said to me, clicking his fingers, while his squared-headed colleague hovered behind. I passed them to him, knowing that I had guilt written all over my face. He considered my card carefully, glancing from the photograph to me and back again, his eyes narrowing. I tried to calm my nerves conscious of the sweat forming on my brow. 'Why are you going to Saint-Romain?'

'To visit—'

'The real reason.'

My stomach caved in. I didn't know what to say.

'Well?'

It was the woman who spoke next – in German, talking quickly.

He considered her words for a few moments, bowed in a slightly exaggerated fashion, and exited, pushing away his colleague, who slid the door firmly shut behind him.

The woman looked at me again, without expression. I wasn't sure what to say. If I thanked her it would only confirm my guilt. What had she said to them, I wondered.

We sat in silence as before – me pretending to read the score, she gazing out of the window. I knew I was far from safe – I still had to run the gauntlet of getting past the guards at the station.

Finally, the train began slowing down – we were approaching Saint-Romain. She stretched her arms and took a deep breath. I realised then that she too was getting off here. I returned the music to my satchel.

20

The station came into view, a much larger place than our local one, boasting several platforms with trains coming and going. We both stood. While checking the contents of her briefcase, she spoke: 'As we pass the guards on the platform, you'll have to walk beside me. Have your documents ready. Say nothing.'

I nodded. Clicking shut her briefcase, she waited for me to open the door.

The platform here was far busier – lots of people, both French and German, some with heavy baggage, boarding, a few alighting. A porter rushed passed us, pushing a trolley laden with suitcases, a newspaper vendor enjoyed a brisk trade, as did a kiosk selling tobacco and sweets. The woman strode briskly, sidestepping others, while I tried to keep up. At the far end of the platform, I could see the barrier decked with swastika flags and manned by numerous Nazis in their ugly uniforms, with Alsatian dogs straining on their leashes. It was a foreboding sight. They had stepped up their presence since the last time I'd been here. I knew I could never have done this alone, and I was relieved to have my new-found companion at my side. We had to queue for some time as the guards ahead of us were stopping everyone and frisking them and searching their bags. I looked round for a bin in which I could ditch my incriminating envelope. The woman, sensing

21

my concern, looked at me and mouthed, 'Don't worry,' before staring straight ahead again.

Slowly, we reached the head of the queue. My companion passed over her documents and signalled me to do the same. Again, she spoke to them in that same authoritative voice in German, and again, whatever she said, did the trick. The guard bowed, returned her papers and indicated to his colleagues to let us through. No one, apart from one of the dogs, even bothered to look at me. We were through to the main part of the station with its high, curved roof and the hustle and bustle of so many people. I felt a surge of relief, almost of adrenalin. This time, in my enthusiasm, I did thank her.

'Please, do not say another word.'

'I'm sorry.'

I think she may have smiled a moment. 'This is where we part.'

'Yes.' I offered my hand. She didn't take it.

'Can I ask your name?' I asked, lowering my arm.

'No.' She turned to leave. Before she left me, she stopped and, turning, said, 'I look forward to watching you conduct one day.'

'Yes, I'll…' But she'd gone, disappearing into the crowd.

*

22

So, now I had to find the African woman and deliver my message. It wasn't difficult, she knew someone would be looking for her, and I saw her, a large, short black woman in her railway uniform with its peaked cap, carrying a pile of envelopes. She watched me as I approached her.

'Can you tell me the time of the next train to Rennes, please?' These were the words I was told to say.

'Not for at least another two hours, Monsieur.' And those were the words I was told would be said back to me. 'Follow me,' she said, in her thick African accent. She led me to the back end of a newspaper kiosk, checking round her in, what I thought, a rather obvious fashion. 'Have you got something for me?' I think she said.

'I'm sorry?'

She rolled her eyes. 'Are you not listening? I said–'

'Oh, yes.' I fished the envelope from my satchel and passed it her.

'Good,' she said, inserting my envelope into the middle of her pile. Without another word, she spun on her shoes and walked briskly away.

'Thank you very much,' I muttered under my breath. Nonetheless, I was hugely relieved to be shot of the offending document. Now, at last, I could breathe easy. I saw her enter an office with the words *Personnel Seulement* written on the door.

I sauntered towards the station exit. Two French policemen stood either side, eyeing the crowds. Above the large doors was a framed portrait of Marshal Pétain, the head of our collaborationist government, bordered by a couple of French flags. I stopped to check the address of my piano teacher on a slip of paper, while people rushed past me. A mother, carrying a small but bulging suitcase, yelled at her child to hurry up; two men bumped into each other, and had started arguing. 'Why don't you look where you're going,' said the taller one, scooping up his hat off the ground. A station announcement broadcast the time of the next train on platform two; two men on ladders were affixing a new poster on the station wall.

I was about to leave, when I heard another commotion behind me. The door to the station office was open. I saw the back of a German uniform; I heard shouts in German-accented French, competing with the argument between the two Frenchmen who had clashed into each other. Had something happened to my African woman? I had to see if anything was wrong. Approaching, I heard a German say, 'We can do this here or you come with us to HQ – it's up to you.' Others, like me, had come to see what was happening. We could see inside, the African women, dwarfed by two German officers, unable to escape their clutches. She caught my eye, her expression one of confusion and fear. One of the Germans followed her gaze. He saw me and the two of us remained frozen for a second, staring at each other. Then, instinctively, I ran. I heard the German yell, 'Hey, you, stop.'

The two French policemen had heard it too but they had moved away from the exit, having become embroiled with the two men arguing. I sprinted out of the station, zigzagging past people, porters and pigeons, and ran down the street, pursued by a number of men in uniforms. 'Out of the way, out of the way,' I heard one shout. 'Stop right now,' screamed another. I turned up a street on my right, running across the road. A car screeched to a halt, the driver sounding his horn. I had no idea where I was; I only knew I had to keep going. 'Stop or we'll fire!' A warning shot rang out. People in the street screamed. A mother pulled her child in as she pinned herself against a wall. I knew the second shot would be aimed at me. I had no choice and came to a halt, putting my hands in the air, my chest heaving as I tried to catch my breath. I refused to turn around but I heard their heavy boots on the tarmac rapidly approaching me. One of them pushed me against a baker's door, my face slammed against the glass. 'You're fast,' he said, breathlessly as his colleagues caught up, 'but not fast enough.' He thrust his revolver into my back. 'Up against the wall. Legs apart.'

25

The baker waved at me from within the shop while a second German began frisking me, his fat hands inside my jacket, against my shirt, checking every pocket. Grabbing me by the shoulder, he turned me around. 'Open your bag.' There were three of them, their revolvers drawn.

'Is this code?' he asked, holding up the score.

'No, it's sheet music – Wagner. He's German.'

'Mm. You've got nothing on you,' said the second once he'd turned my satchel inside out. 'So why are you running away, eh? What are you hiding?'

'Nothing.'

'Nothing? You run away for nothing?'

'I'm in a hurry.'

'Don't try to be funny. Right, you're coming with us.'

'But I haven't done anything wrong.'

'We'll soon see about that.'

Passers-by stopped to stare as I was marched back to the train station, my hands still above my head, my three Germans behind me. Those coming towards me stepped off the pavement to let me pass, concerned looks upon their faces. An older woman in black winked. Perhaps she thought I was some sort of a hero.

We were almost back at the station when I heard what was now a familiar voice shouting in German. 'Halt,' said one

26

of the soldiers.

And there she was — the woman from the train, berating the Germans while showing them her ID. They passed it from one to the other as she launched into a long tale, speaking quickly in that authoritative tone.

One responded in a quiet voice. The exchange continued in German while I watched them daring to hope that I'd get away from this.

The Germans answered as one, sounding apologetic. Turning to me, the woman said, 'I've explained to the gentlemen and they realise they've made a mistake. You're free to go.'

I opened my mouth not sure what to say or how to thank her.

'Accept our apologies, Monsieur,' said one of the soldiers.

'Oh, yes. Easy mistake to make,' I said with a confidence I didn't feel.

I bowed to the woman and even clicked my heels. 'Thank you, Madame.'

I quickly returned back to the station. Stuff my piano teacher, I thought; I was heading back home.

Paris, November 1966

The inside of the theatre is almost dark, just a few wall lights shining dimly. The orchestra waits in silence, their instruments at the ready. The audience, likewise silent, await with anticipation. Someone coughs but otherwise a hush has descended. The air is tense with expectation. I stand in the wings and collect myself. I take a deep breath. Unconsciously, I tap my baton against my leg but I am not nervous; I'm too good for that, but still, I sense the adrenaline building within me, seeping through my veins. The stage manager gives me the nod. It is time. I step out. A spotlight falls on me, traces my steps onto the stage. The audience erupts into enthusiastic applause. I reach the podium. I turn and face the audience. I take a deep bow. The audience applauds with even greater enthusiasm. Then, I turn and face my orchestra. Slowly, bit by bit, the audience falls silent again. The hush is even more intense now. I tap my baton against the music stand. The

28

orchestra look at me, awaiting my command. It is time to begin.

A conductor bears a huge weight of responsibility – a poor conductor can render a magnificent work mediocre, reduce an esteemed orchestra to that of a confused rabble, and can flaw even the greatest of singers. The composer, who has spent possibly years writing and perfecting his work is then entirely in the hands of the conductor who brings it to life. They say that even Beethoven, blighted by his deafness, ruined his own work as a conductor. The orchestra is as dependent upon their conductor as a newly-born child is dependent upon its mother.

Conducting an eighty-piece orchestra in the confines of a recording studio is a very different prospect to a live venue. One feels restrained; it is not a natural setting. In a live situation, the conductor and musicians feed off the audience and the environment; there is a natural energy that spurs us on to higher deeds, to a greater performance. Not so in a studio, with its muted, artificial air. All spontaneity is destroyed. As a conductor one must spur one's charges to produce a music that is beyond mere workmanship. Theoretically, a studio recording allows one to stop and re-record as much or as little as necessary; it provides one with the opportunity to attain perfection. Yet, in reality, it does exactly the opposite – it acts as a stop on creativity, it renders both the musicians and the conductor too self-conscious. We follow the music, not our hearts. Therefore, one has to work ten times harder to try to produce a work that is worthy of one's name and the composer's expectations.

Then, from the recording studio to the editing suite, where technology plays its part, where one can lift a performance to something near what one hears in the head. At the end of the process, one is left with a perfect rendition, perfect but soulless. My first studio recording, with my new Parisian orchestra, was Brahms's First Symphony. It almost caused me to suffer a breakdown, not least because I carried the burden of expectation. The orchestra and I had been signed up by a big American record label. They expected great things from us, and from me in particular; they expected a return on their investment. I had a recording budget which, although on paper might have seemed generous, was never going to be enough. In the end, it was money, not time, that forced me to declare the work finished. The label executives were delighted, congratulating me on such a fine piece of work. I accepted their thanks with dignity while I suffered sleepless nights knowing full well that I had not even begun to capture the work as I had intended.

I spent a day being photographed for the record sleeve.

My good looks, they said, would help shift sales. Shift? Words failed me. Was I selling a cereal, I asked them. They insisted and I had no choice. But, I'll admit, the final result was impressive – me with my hands in the air, gripping my baton, the glow of artistic perspiration on my brow.

Then came the day of release – I expected the worst, and wished I had been selling cereals after all. I need not have worried – it sold beyond expectations. I finished with the year's bestselling classical release in all France. My name was known the country over. My American bosses were delighted; my bank manager and my wife even more so. French record companies, who had failed to secure me, outbid by their American competitors, hinted at my lack of patriotism.

The following year, I was back in the studio – several times. The Americans had their golden goose and they were going to make damned sure they made the most of it. I never did learn to enjoy working in a studio, but I quickly learnt to enjoy the fruits of my labour. Michèle and I bought a grand new home in an affluent southern suburb of Paris, far bigger than we needed. I bought two fine cars, new clothes, the latest gadgets and innovations. My recordings won prizes, I was interviewed, my face appeared on the front of magazines; I was asked to endorse various products, enhancing my income even further.

Michèle and I had married in 1949. A subdued affair; I was still the conductor of a small, provincial orchestra, and my pay was meagre. Michèle was its violist. But, unlike me, music was not her obsession; it never permeated to her marrow. She played moderately well and music was a means by which to earn an income. The viola was, to her, merely the tool of her trade. She was petite with heavy eyelids, a sharp nose, dimpled cheeks and a most pleasant smile. She too had been in the resistance but a much more active member than me. She'd been arrested and brutally tortured by the Gestapo. She had a number of scars that criss-crossed her back. She never told me the details suffice to say that, as a result, she'll never have children. Such was my love for her, I didn't mind. Alas, I always felt that our love was rather one-sided, that the Gestapo, as well as leaving the scars, had also stripped her of her ability to love. When I met her in Paris in the days following liberation, she had been so vibrant, her zest for life infectious. She was 'someone', she had influence, men listened to her. But after the war, once things began to settle, she seemed to lose her way and nothing I did or said helped. Peace seemed so dull for her; it was as if she needed war to feel alive.

Seventeen years on and I was at the top of my career. Things could not have gone better. It never occurred to me, not even for a moment, that it might all, one day, pop like a

32

balloon. It was in Paris, November sixty-six. I'd just conducted Mahler's Fifth, always an exhausting affair, when I received a visitor. I was in my dressing room, backstage at the *Salle Pleyel*, still wearing my tuxedo, my bowtie undone. It was one of those traditional dressing rooms with light bulbs around the mirror. On the dresser in front of me, a bottle of champagne in a bucket of ice, half empty; I'd already consumed three glasses in quick succession. I was sprawled back in my chair, still catching my breath, replaying the music in my head, smiling inanely at my reflection and congratulating myself on another success when there was a knock on the door. 'Would Maestro be prepared to accept a visitor?' asked a pale member of the theatre staff. 'Would it be convenient?'

'No,' I said, catching sight of her in the mirror. 'Any interviews have to be arranged with my agent.' I really couldn't face another reporter or music reviewer at this moment.

The young woman bowed and, closing the door, disappeared.

I poured myself another glass of champagne and, holding it aloft, toasted my reflection. The evening could not have gone better. Well, there was one thing but I'd long ago given up on that. Michèle never came to my concerts. She did to begin with, years back, when I was still relatively unknown. But since I'd become famous, she preferred to stay away. She didn't enjoy the limelight, she said, all the attention. I didn't understand it. The attention, the limelight, was on *me*, not her. Did she not want to share my triumphs; rejoice in my success? No. Sadly not. She didn't. I'd return home, exhausted by the evaporating adrenalin, and find her in bed, asleep. Admittedly, it was always very late, but still, after such excitement, such adulation, returning home to a quiet, darkened house, was akin to having a bucket of cold water thrown over me.

There was another knock on the door. 'What is it now?' I shouted.

The member of the theatre staff, now even paler, popped her head round the door. 'I'm terribly sorry to disturb you again, Maestro, but this visitor is most insistent. She says she simply has to see you.'

I sighed heavily, still staring at my reflection. 'God damn it,' I said under my breath. Then louder, 'OK, I give in; show her in, whoever she is.'

'Yes, Maestro. Thank you.'

This had better be good, I thought, finishing off my glass of champagne. A few seconds passed. Then I heard the tread of heavy footsteps on the carpeted corridor outside my dressing room. A knock on the door.

'Enter.'

'Good evening, Maestro,' said the stranger behind me.

I spun round in my chair. I opened my mouth to say something but the words stuck in my throat. Standing in front of me was not a reporter, not a reviewer, but the woman from the train all those years ago. She looked smart in a tailored mackintosh and a silk scarf. She'd aged a little, after all it'd been twenty years, *in 1966* a few lines on her face, her black hair, now much longer, was streaked with grey, but otherwise she looked much the same.

'Have you got time?'

'Yes, of course,' I said, almost falling out of my chair to invite her in. She offered her hand. I took it. 'What a surprise. How... how did you find me?'

She laughed. 'It wasn't difficult – your face is everywhere.'

'I suppose.'

She looked me up and down, seeing what time had done to me in the intervening years. 'You look well. You're doing well.'

'Yes, perhaps. I'm sorry – do take a seat.' I offered her my chair in front of the mirror but instead she sat in the little chair in the corner of the room.

'This will do fine,' she said, looking slightly absurd as she nestled her bottom on the tiny seat.

'Can I get you a drink? Champagne perhaps?'

'No, no, I don't want to take up your time.'

35

'Did you… I mean, were you here for the concert?'

'Oh yes. In fact, I've been to several. I've been following your career with interest. I always remember our conversation on the train. You said that one day you'd be a conductor. I may have doubted you. For that, I apologise, for here you are. Not only a conductor but the most famous one in France. I congratulate you.'

Usually, I can take compliments in my stride, I was well practised by now, but this time I felt genuinely bashful. 'Thank you. And you, Madam, you look well.'

'I am, thank you. I never did tell you my name. Let me introduce myself – *Mademoiselle* Lapointe. You must call me Hilda.'

'And my name is–'

'Oh, I know your name. The whole country knows your name by now.'

'Ha, you make me sound like one of The Beatles.'

'Oh, please, Maestro, there's no need to compare yourself to those delinquents and their Negro music.'

I didn't like to say I rather admired the four boys from across The Channel. 'Mademoiselle Lapointe–'

'Hilda, please.'

'Hilda – I still, after all these years, appreciate how you helped me that day. I've never forgotten it. I admit, I was carrying some papers that… well, if they'd been discovered…'

'Would have been compromising?' *executed*

I smiled. 'Yes, exactly.'

'It's all water under the bridge now.'

'Yes. Yes, it is.'

We sat in silence for a while, remembering a time that seemed so distant and so alien to seem unreal now.

I cleared my throat. 'Would you care, Mademoiselle, Hilda, for a spot to eat? There are so many—'

She held up her hand. 'No, no. It's very kind of you, Maestro, but no. I just wanted to…' She rose to her feet. Rearranging her scarf, she said, 'I don't know — to say hello, I suppose, and to say how pleased I am that things have turned out so well for you.'

'Well, thank you. If it hadn't been for you, it could have turned out very differently.' She seemed pleased with that; pleased with the acknowledgement. 'But what I've always wanted to know, is what exactly did you say to them?' *did not tell she was speaking in German*

'Let's just say I used my powers of persuasion.'

'Yes, but what—'

'I must go. It's been lovely seeing you again.' We shook hands again, and I showed her out of the door and passed her to the theatre boy to escort her back outside.

Closing the door, I slunk in my chair and smiled at my

reflection. Yes, I thought, perhaps if she hadn't intervened all those years ago, if she hadn't offered her protection, things might well have turned out very differently.

I poured myself another glass of champagne and toasted myself and my continued success. It was late. Time, I decided, to order a car to take me home.

August 1942

Back during the war

Following my close escape at the railway station, I stayed at home, not wanting to venture out for fear I might bump into Monsieur Gapon. My mother became concerned for me, asking if I was alright. 'It's not natural for a young man never to go out.' She told me my skin looked pasty and that I needed some air. As it was, about a week later, Monsieur Gapon came to the door. I didn't know he knew my address.

'Unfortunate business with the African woman,' he said, glancing up and down the street. He had a flat nose as if someone had punched it, and small eyes that never stopped moving. Monsieur Gapon was a farmer and somehow he carried the smell of dung with him. It was obvious he wanted to be invited in but I resisted. I didn't want the man inside my home, polluting it somehow.

'What happened to her?' I asked if only for the sake of appearance. The truth is, I didn't want to know, didn't want to be drawn further into his orbit.

He shrugged. 'The way I see it, she was either careless or, worse...'

'Yes?'

'We have a rat in our ranks.'

'Oh.'

Now he looked at me with a hard expression. 'And if we find out who that rat is, mark my words, his life won't be worth living.' He drew a finger across his throat. I gulped. 'Now, listen, I've got another job for you.'

'Oh? Well...'

'A bit more dangerous this time.'

'Ah, well, yes. Listen, Monsieur, I'd love to but I can't at the moment. You see...'

He cocked his head.

'Well, you see it's my mother. She's... she's very poorly at the moment.'

'It won't take you long.'

'Oh, but I can't leave her, the... the d-doctor said. He-he said I shouldn't leave her. Not even for a minute.'

He peered over my shoulder, trying to see in his house. 'Is she dying?'

'Well. No. Yes. I, er, I don't know.'

He shook his head, threw me a disdainful look and strode off.

40

The occupation carried on around me but I tried not to let it impinge on my life. I was frequently stopped by an official pair of Germans as I went about my business and asked for my identity card, but apart from that I was free to pursue my interest in music. Frankly I was more worried about Monsieur Gapon than the Boche. I was desperate to leave my sleepy village. My mother irritated me, and my father had died when I was young. I felt no ties to the place and wanted so much to go out and explore the world. But I learnt to be patient – I knew my time would come. I may have lost my place at music college, but I went to see my piano teacher in Saint-Romain. Occasionally, I played a recital at the local church. Starved of entertainment, it always attracted a good turnout, including a number of appreciative Germans. I would never have said this aloud, but frankly, the Germans had a better understanding of music than our local philistines.

A month or so later, Monsieur Gapon returned. 'How's your mother?' he asked, the smell of dung assaulting my nostrils.

'Oh, not so good.'

'Funny that. She seemed well when I saw in the market yesterday.'

'Oh yes, yes, she can walk about now but, you know, she gets tired very easily. I have to make sure–'

'Good, well, now she's up and about, I've got a job for you.'

'I can't, Monsieur. Much as I want to do my bit, I have a… a piano exam coming up.'

'A piano exam?' he said, enunciating the words slowly.

I felt my face go red. 'Yes, it's terribly important, you see.'

He put his hand up. 'Forget it. If your *piano exam* is more important than the future of our nation, then I have no time for you.' He turned to leave but, alas, stopped. Jabbing his fat finger into my chest, he said, 'Don't think I'm gonna forget this. When the day of liberation comes, you watch your back, young man.'

My mouth opened and shut, like a fish fighting for air. But before I could think of something to say, he'd gone.

I only saw Monsieur Gapon once more. Indeed, I was the very last person he ever set eyes on. It was about two months later, November 1942. I was in the open-air market, doing some shopping for my mother. We were perpetually hungry, food was in short supply. All the things we took for granted before the war were now a distant memory – meat, poultry, eggs, cheese, fish. What little there was was siphoned off by the Boche or known collaborators. All I had in my string bag, were a couple of potatoes and a battered onion. A bitter wind, funnelled down the passageways between the rows of stalls, biting into me. I was watching a stallholder juggling three potatoes when we heard a disturbance nearby. Someone was running, I could see him through the market stalls, zigzagging past shoppers in the adjacent passageway, pushing people aside. 'Hell,' I said aloud. 'It's Monsieur Gapon.' And chasing him, just a few feet behind, were two Germans.

Gapon turned the corner and came lumbering up between the stalls heading towards me. He was no runner. The Germans were catching up.

'Halt,' shouted one of the Germans. The other, turning the corner, stopped and, lifting his rifle to his shoulder, took aim. People screamed, threw themselves between the stalls. I stood stock still, paralysed. Gapon had almost reached me when I heard the loud crack. He threw his head back, his arms flailing and staggered a few paces. He stopped, panting, and looked up straight at me. I stepped back, frightened by the intensity of his eyes when the second gunshot felled him. He lay in a heap at my feet, a stream of blood already pooling around his head. The German soldiers shouted at people to stay back as they reached him. They began arguing with one another, one pushing the other. The stallholder, who had ducked beneath his stall, re-emerged, chuckling. 'They weren't meant to kill him,' he said quietly, explaining their argument.

Paris, August 1944

Paris was liberated in August 1944, the Nazis finally driven out. We were free at last! Immediately, I bade my mother farewell, said goodbye to my sleepy village and headed for the capital. I was there at the centre of it all, drinking in the celebratory atmosphere. It felt as if the whole nation had converged on the Champs-Élysées and danced and jumped up and down with happiness as the sun shone down on us. What a carnival; I'd never experienced such joy. People clung onto lamp posts, leaned out of windows, stood on roofs. We sang the *Marseillaise* again and again. We watched and toasted the American tanks on the streets and cheered the soldiers. Wow, they seemed a breed apart, so handsome and slick with their white teeth and chewing gum. No wonder our girls threw themselves at them. *Vive l'Amérique!* The atmosphere was contagious; never had I seen people so happy. But the biggest attraction was the appearance of our hero, the nation's saviour,

General de Gaulle. People surged forward to catch a glimpse of the man. It wasn't difficult – he was so tall, his little pointed cap perched at the back of his head. He walked briskly down the Champs-Élysées, the Arc de Triomphe behind them. He walked purposefully, a man claiming his destiny, looking around, his head up, as if sniffing the air. Men in suits surrounded him, a motorcycle and sidecar, while photographers jostled with each other to keep pace, taking their photographs. *Vive De Gaulle!*

A petite woman with dimpled cheeks and short, almost black hair stepped on my toes. 'Oh my.' She laughed. 'I'm so sorry.' She leaned up and planted a kiss on my cheek.

'Hey, hey, what's your name?'

'Michèle,' she said, before being swept away by the surging crowd.

That evening, I fell in with a group of students, made friends, drank, went to parties and waved the flag. I shared my story of resistance, inventing a whole new persona for myself. I tried blocking the image if Monsieur Gapon from my mind. No one doubted me for a moment.

They were giddy times. After four years of occupation, the future seemed unending with possibility and awash with opportunity.

The following day, walking down a narrow boulevard

ehind the Champs-Élysées, completely enveloped in shade, I saw a group of people ahead in a small square, gathering in front of a fountain, shouting and calling out the vilest of names. I joined the throng. At the centre of it, was a women accused of having slept with Germans, a 'horizontal collaborator', as they were known. She was about the same age as me. She stood, impassive, her arms hanging limply at her sides while two men hacked at her hair, cutting it all off. Curls of blonde hair gathered at her feet. The dulled, resigned expression on her face reminded me of the images of Mary Magdalene kneeling at the feet of the crucified Jesus. People laughed and clapped and pointed at her shaven head, calling it the new hairstyle of '44. They shouted traitor, bitch, whore. People stepped up and spat at her. I heard a woman shout, 'Serves you right for being a mattress for the Boche, you slut.' Then, once the men had finished with their scissors, a woman approached her from behind and yanked down her shirt, the buttons popping, leaving the woman exposed in just her brassiere. A man stepped forward and wielding a paintbrush, branded her chest with a swastika. The poor woman didn't move, seemed impervious to it all.

Then a woman's loud voice, cutting through the laughter and mirth. 'Stop this, stop this now.' I saw the crowd part as this new woman pushed her way through. 'Leave her alone.'

46

People mumbled and jeered at her yet they seemed to accept her command. She took Mary Magdalene's hand. 'You should be ashamed of yourselves.' I had to stand on my tiptoes to catch a glimpse of this woman. It was her, the woman who'd stepped on my toes the day before, Michèle.

She may have been short, but boy, she had some authority. Slowly, reluctantly, the crowd dispersed. I also turned to leave but then I stopped. Could I go and say hello to her, this woman who seemed to have so much sway?

I stepped forward, fearfully. She caught my eye fleetingly but didn't recognise me. She scanned the area, making sure peace was restored. 'Hello again,' I said.

Both women looked at me, Mary and Michèle. Michèle narrowed her eyes.

'We… we met yesterday. You stepped on my shoes?'

She glared at me and I was already regretting my bravado but then she burst out laughing. 'Oh yes, so I did. Come on, you can help me get this young lady home.'

Paris, May 1968

After years of recording and performing, of going on concert and promotional tours, I needed a break. The novelty of fame and the strain of being in constant demand had begun to take its toll. I was due to start work soon on a live performance and a new recording of Berlioz's Second Symphony, along with some supplementary pieces. But first, Michèle and I went on holiday to Morocco. I fell in love with Moroccan music with its erratic rhythms and earthy roots. We spent hours browsing round the souks of Marrakech, buying knick-knacks, drinking strong coffee, eating tagines, indulging the street children and their nuisance. After a week, we relaxed on the coast, going on camel rides, boat trips, reading and idling the hours away in the local cafés. I thought that perhaps, just perhaps, my wife had begun to learn how to love.

We returned to find Paris in a state of turmoil. People had taken to the streets, fighting the police, overturning cars, building barricades. Revolution was in the air as demonstrators preached liberty and socialism. Students occupied their universities, workers downed tools. President de Gaulle teetered. The country was in a state of anarchy. Public transport, postal services, the whole infrastructure crumbled.

I was at work, having begun rehearsals on the Berlioz, when, one morning in early May, a small delegation of students came to see me – earnest, young men and women, with long hair and high ideals. They wanted me to speak on their behalf, my fame would give the movement credibility, they said. I wasn't sure – I was an establishment figure and rocking the boat had never been my thing. But they were so persuasive and motivated – how could I turn them down? I admired the strength of their convictions and their belief in the justice of their cause. I realised how blinkered I'd been all my life. Michèle was dead set against it. I'd be risking my career, she said, I'd be setting my stall against the very people, the conservatives and the elite, who saw me as one of their own. And what, she asked, would the record label make of it? They paid me to make music, not to bring down governments. I told her not to be so dramatic; the students had legitimate concerns, they had principles; who was I to turn my back on them? I knew the real reason – I'd been given the chance to atone for the guilt I felt at my lack of gumption during the war.

I did wonder why they had approached me. There were many far more suitable men in the public eye who would have made a better spokesman for their cause than me. It didn't take long to find out. The orchestra had recently recruited a new cellist, a talented young woman named Isabelle. She had long, dark hair, often decorated with a little bow, wide puppy-dog eyes, thin, painfully so, and fine cheekbones. She was also earnest, impressionistic and idealistic – she was one of them. She'd approached me one day, holding hands as she spoke to me with a sandal-wearing, long-haired, bearded youth I presumed to be her boyfriend. She introduced him as Jacques. I said I'd already been asked and was considering it.

The following day, after rehearsals, I called her over and told her yes, I would do it.

'Thank you,' she said, almost skipping with enthusiasm. For a moment I thought she was about to hug me. 'I hope you're not cross with me for asking.'

'No, no, not at all.'

'We all thought you'd be such a good choice. People will listen to you.'

'Am I not too conservative for you?'

'No, you're old enough to remember the war and to have witnessed its injustices but you're young enough, just about, to still be relevant.'

50

I thanked her for this backhanded compliment.

'So, how are you enjoying your work?' I asked.

'I love it. I've always wanted to work for you, Maestro. It's a dream come true for me,' she said, grinning.

'Good. You play well. More importantly, you know how to listen. I've noticed this.' I asked how old she was, where she'd come from, where she'd studied. Questions I'd asked when I interviewed her, but this time I listened. She reminded me of myself as a 22-year-old – confident, aware of her own abilities, and what she wanted from life. She was certainly attractive, if rather thin for my liking, but I had no intention of being unfaithful to my wife just as things were changing for the better. Anyway, she had a boyfriend, the bearded, Jesus-like chap I'd met the day before – a student, she told me, at the Sorbonne.

It was a fine spring day, when, surrounded by thousands of students and workers, I stood on a platform to the side of a park and was handed a loudhailer. Nearby, two upturned cars lay smouldering, thin veils of smoke adding to the surreal atmosphere of a city under siege. I was nervous – this was to be the most frightening performance of my life so far. In front of me, a sea of expectant faces, banners held aloft plastered with revolutionary slogans. I spotted Isabelle, her arms linked with her student boyfriend. She gave me a little wave. I tried to smile. Policemen with riot gear kept a careful eye on us. I mumbled through my speech, written for me by one of the student leaders, criticising the state for treating its citizens like children, demanding greater social justice, a greater share of the prosperity produced by the masses but enjoyed by the few. I understood little of what I read; I knew nothing about these things. Reporters took notes; photographers did their work. I realised that I may have been a great conductor but I was no talker. Yet, my speech was greatly applauded and cheered, and as I descended the platform, I was greeted with appreciative slaps on the back, and hearty thanks from those who had organised the demonstration.

'Well done, Maestro, that was great.' It was Isabelle. I wondered whether she was being entirely honest. Her boyfriend, Jacques, invited me to a meeting. I thanked him but said no – I had done enough revolutionising for one day. I knew my performance had been below par but, nonetheless, relieved it was over, I returned home in a state of high excitement. Even Michèle's rebukes didn't blunt my enthusiasm. The deeper understanding we'd gained of one another, forged in Morocco, had already evaporated, and we'd quickly returned to our normal selves – acknowledging each other's presence but maintaining a perpetual distance. I only realised, many years later, that my insistence on helping the demonstrators had so annoyed my wife that it had destroyed whatever small stirrings of affection we'd found in Marrakech.

The following day, unusually for me, I bought a newspaper and was surprised to see a picture of myself at the bottom of the front page. *Has the Maestro lost his marbles?* screamed the headline. The article made for grim reading: *He may be able to lift a baton and lead an orchestra of talented musicians, but the Maestro's attempts to lead the masses on a merry dance of revolution fell on deaf ears yesterday. He mumbled through a speech ridden with clichés and empty rhetoric that would have embarrassed a ten-year-old. The Maestro may be a demon on the rostrum but as a rebel he is as effective as a decrepit church mouse. Stick to what you know, Maestro. The students can mess it up just as easily without you!* I just hoped the article didn't echo Isabelle's opinion.

I threw the paper away; I had no wish for Michèle to find it. Nevertheless, I followed the progress of the demonstrations with a keen interest, buying various newspapers everyday and exclaiming at the papers' pro-establishment stance and the scorn they heaped upon the demonstrators. Despite the drubbing I received, I felt the urge to join them at the barricades. But I resisted it. I didn't want to push my luck too far with my American bosses. A pity, for I felt that for the first time in my life, I had found a purpose that wasn't solely based around me. It was during this euphoric time, however, that I received the letter.

I had a secretary that dealt with my post, and my travel arrangements and appointments. She had a stack of postcards featuring a sombre black-and-white photograph of me, an official shot taken in a studio, and signed by her with my name. She answered my fan mail and batted off all but the most important correspondence. This letter she deemed worthy enough of my personal attention. Postmarked locally, it read:

My dear Maestro,

A huge misfortune has fallen on me. I know you are terribly busy and I wouldn't normally bother you unless it was extremely important. I have been arrested and accused of all sorts of fanciful things.

I desperately need your help.

I ask you to remember our short journey together on the train to Saint-Romain all those years ago. Please, Maestro, if you could contact my lawyer, M. d'Espérey, on the telephone number above, he's expecting to hear from you.

I beseech you to help me in my hour of need.

Yours sincerely,

Hilda Lapointe (Mademoiselle).

I re-read it several times. I knew I had no choice – I had to respond. If nothing else, I was intrigued; I had to know.

'*Accused of all sorts of fanciful things.*' I rang Monsieur d'Espérey, her lawyer, but he told me little except that his client had been arrested and was due to stand trial. He asked me to come see him at his offices in the sixteenth *arrondissement* but to keep it to myself and not to tell anyone. No fear of that, I thought; I certainly had no intention of telling Michèle.

At eleven o'clock the following day, I found myself in the offices of *Messieurs d'Espérey et Cotillard*, a plush office on the fourth floor of an ornate nineteenth century block, with red leather armchairs and a mahogany desk and a brass lamp. Sitting behind the desk in a pinstriped suit was Monsieur d'Espérey, a man in his sixties with a thin, grey moustache and rimless glasses sliding off the end of his nose.

'I believe you know my client, Mademoiselle Lapointe?' he said, in a baritone voice.

'I wouldn't say I *know* her – I've only met her twice. And that was over a course of twenty years or so.'

He considered this for a few moments. 'Nonetheless, I understand she, how shall we say, she helped you out once. During the war. Got you out of an awkward situation,' he said with upturned palms.

'Well, yes.'

'Can you describe this occasion?'

I did, relating briefly our encounter on the train during

the years of occupation. He listened intently, his head tilted to the side.

After I'd finished, he scribbled a few words on a notepad on his desk. 'Good.'

'Is it?'

He looked up at me. 'Oh yes, it'll help. My client is due to appear in court on the second of June. We will enter a not guilty plea, after which we will be assigned a date for trial. Probably sometime in September. My client and I have no illusions, she is likely to be found guilty but it is the sentence that concerns us. I would like you, if you would agree, to stand as a character witness. If she is sentenced, your testimony could help lessen the severity of the punishment.'

'I – I don't understand. I don't know what Mademoiselle Lapointe has been arrested for.'

He threw his hands in the air. 'I apologise. I assumed… no matter. Mademoiselle Lapointe, my client, is standing trial for war crimes…'

I swallowed. 'War crimes?'

'Yes, during her time at the Drancy camp, particularly in her treatment of its Jewish inmates.'

I stared at him, goggled-eyed. 'Drancy? Wasn't that…?'

'A concentration camp right here in our city – yes. You had no idea she was a camp guard?'

I shook my head, speechless.

'OK, let me brief you. You understand this is all highly confidential. If you were to—'

'I understand.'

'Very well then.' He sighed before launching into the tale. 'Mademoiselle Lapointe worked as a guard at the Drancy internment camp from June 1942 until its liberation in August 1944. I don't know how much you know, but the Vichy wartime government carted off Jews, both foreign born and French, to Drancy where they were interned in appalling conditions before being deported to the death camps in the east, mainly Auschwitz. Some seventy thousand were sent. Very few returned.'

'I remember now,' I said quietly.

'I think we are all aware of it; it's just that not many of us want to think about it. We deliberately want to forget; it is too much of a stain on our memory. Like any job, Mademoiselle Lapointe, or Irène d'Urville as she was then, started at a lowly position at the camp but with time, she was promoted. However, after the war, she managed to disappear. She changed her name, lived in the south for a while. She was small fry – it wasn't difficult. However, she was discovered, just recently, quite by chance.'

'But… I thought you said she was not guilty.'

57

remanded

'She's not denying that she worked there but she denies the charges levelled against her – that she meted out unfair and brutal punishment on inmates.'

'I see. Monsieur d'Espérey, I won't be able to attend on June second; I have—'

'That doesn't matter. As long as you are available to give your testimony. That's when it matters.'

'OK, I'll be there. Can I visit Hilda?'

'Of course. She's been remanded on bail. I don't want to give out her home address, so leave it with me. I'll arrange something.'

*

Monsieur d'Espérey was a man true to his word. A week later I found myself sitting opposite Hilda in a small, rundown café within sight of the Sacré-Cœur. Despite its advantageous location, the place was nearly deserted as we sipped our coffees. With untreated brick walls, uncomfortable chairs, wilting plants and sullen staff, the lawyer couldn't have found us a more dingy place had he tried. 'Come here often?' I joked.

Hilda didn't laugh. She looked like a woman under strain. Gone was the blustery woman who had come to my dressing room two years before; here was a thinner, older-looking woman in a drab, blue-grey cardigan, her hair scraped back,

58

her eyes dulled.

'I went to see your lawyer. He told me the story, well, the outline of it. What happened, Mademoiselle?'

She gazed beyond me to the world outside.

'So, that's how you got me through that day – you were one of them.'

She nodded, still unable to look at me.

'You were one of them,' I repeated for effect.

This time, she reacted, looking straight at me. 'Yes, I was one of them, as you say,' she snapped, leaning forward. 'But I saved you, didn't I? That's the point. I'm painted as this terrible person, as evil personified. And yes, I did some things I'm not proud of. But life isn't always black and white, is it? This is why you must help me now, Maestro. You have to help me.'

'I don't know if it'll make any difference but yes, I told your lawyer, I will speak on your behalf. But you must tell me… something that has puzzled me these last 26 years – why did you help me? I was nothing to you, so why?'

The owner of the café appeared before us, asking whether we wanted a refill of coffee. We both gladly accepted. We waited while he poured fresh, steaming coffee into our mugs and brought us a little jug of hot milk. We thanked him and as he returned to his counter, the café door opened and a young couple holding hands came in, hovered at the door, and backed out. I saw the searing look of disappointment on the owner's face.

'Very well then,' she said eventually. 'I will tell you, then you can judge whether I am as bad as they make out. That day I met you on the train, I was on leave. About the only leave I got while I worked at that place.'

'Drancy?'

She nodded. With her eyes still focused elsewhere, she told me her story. 'I was on my way to visit an old friend of mine in Saint-Romain. You came into that carriage and started reading that sheet music of yours. You were humming the tune aloud – I don't think you were even aware of it. I was impressed. I thought it's so rare to see a youngster practicing such noble pursuits. I thought how proud your parents must be of you. And then, of course, the Germans came in wanting to see our papers. I saw straightaway that you had something to hide – it was written all over your face. Normally, I wouldn't have intervened. I was a collaborator; I freely admit that. It was wrong of me, I know, but at the time I felt I was doing the right thing. You, on the other hand, were clearly working for the resistance.'

'I was only delivering a message.'

'Nonetheless. You were still very young – you hadn't

learnt the art of disguising your body language. I felt sorry for you. Perhaps, deep down, I knew that if they searched you and then arrested you, we would have risked losing one of our finest musicians. I knew, instinctively somehow, that you deserved a second chance. So, it was simple, I showed the guards my Drancy card that stated my job and told them you were with me.'

'As simple as that?'

Now, finally, she looked at me. 'As simple as that. I told them you were a trainee, and again, when they caught you in the street.'

'A *trainee*? In that place?'

'It saved you.'

'I was only a messenger.'

'Maybe, but I wasn't to know that. Still, they would have asked you for names, and I'm sure you know what that would have meant.'

'Yes.' I thought of the boy who did my job before me. Deported to a work camp somewhere in Germany. He never came back. Worked to death at the age of twenty-one.

'Remembering how you were, I don't think you would have withstood it very well.'

'You're right. I doubt I would today.'

'Exactly.'

'What happened after the war? What did you do?'

'It wasn't difficult.' She drummed her fingers on the tabletop. 'There was so much confusion. Accusations and claims and counter-claims, collaborators who pretended to have been in the resistance. I put on some old clothes, made myself look like a peasant woman, and made my way to Saint-Romain, and stayed with my friend there. We became close. She vouched for me and together we invented a new history for myself.'

'And your papers?'

'I told them they'd all been destroyed in the war.'

'Perfectly feasible, I suppose.'

'Oh yes. Lots of people did it.'

'So how were you found out?'

She sighed at the regrettable memory. 'I was recognised. I've been living in Paris a number of years now. I knew there was always the risk and sure enough, one day, I was shopping in a big department store in the centre of town when someone, a horrible little man, a Jew, of course, came up to me and said "Hello, Madame d'Urville", that was my name then, not that I was married. Never have been. Like you on the train, I was unable to hide my reaction. I should have been on my guard. I tried to back away but I knew there was no escape. He yelled the place down. The store manager came down and forcibly took me to his office and from there he called the police. The silly thing is, had I'd been arrested at the time, after the war, I would have been one of many. But now, by myself, I'm exposed. But you know, I am no more than a scapegoat for a country still too ashamed of its wartime guilt to look at itself in the mirror.'

'Is that how you see it?'

'Of course. Yes, we are now a country full of resisters but we all know it's not true. Especially at the beginning of the war – had it been put to the vote, ninety per cent of us would have voted for the collaborationist government. At least I'm being honest. I worked for them; I regret it, of course, but I don't see why I should play the part of the sacrificial lamb.' I tried not to laugh – a scapegoat and a sacrificial lamb. I wondered how many other farmyard animals she could conjure up.

'And I saved you. Can I be that bad?'

'I don't know, Hilda, you tell me. What happened in that place?'

'In Drancy?' She looked away, scanning the café with its empty chairs and unoccupied tables. Behind the counter, the owner polished a glass, a cigarette stuck to his lip. 'We had to maintain discipline. It was war.'

'Discipline?'

'It was not a holiday camp.'

63

'But what do you mean – discipline?'

'So many questions. Am I on trial already?'

'No, Hilda, but you soon will be.'

Paris, September 1968

It'd been a difficult summer. Rehearsals for the Berlioz symphony were arduous and took every ounce of my energy. I returned home at night exhausted and bad-tempered, hoping for some sympathy from my wife, but finding none.

One evening, on my return from a rehearsal, she told me to sit down; there was something she needed to tell me. I did as told, the thumping in my heart warning me that I wasn't going to like this.

'I think...'

'Yes?'

She rubbed her eyes. 'I think we should sleep in separate beds from now on.'

I stared at her, not sure I'd heard her correctly. 'But... But why, Michèle?'

'I just... I think it's for the best.'

'Best for who?'

'I've made up a bed for you in the second bedroom.'

'Already?'

'I'm…' She fished out a handkerchief from her cardigan pocket. 'I'm still fond of you but…'

I waited, watching her twist the handkerchief around her fingers. 'But what, my love? Tell me. Have I done—'

'No. No, you've done nothing wrong. I'm very fond of you, really I am, but I don't love you.'

I don't love you. The words hit me in the gut, one after the other. My mind clouded over, trying to make sense of it, of what she'd said. 'S-surely, y-you don't—'

'And I don't think I ever did.'

My mouth went dry. She sat there but I couldn't see her properly, the glaze of tears over my eyes too thick.

'I'm sorry,' she said.

Sorry? Was that it? She was sorry?

With no sense of what I was doing, I rose. I held onto the side of the settee, fearing I might fall without support. I took a deep breath and tried momentarily to gather myself. 'I accept your apology.'

I bowed, left the room, retired to bed and sobbed.

*

The riots had finished – the workers returned to work and the students went back to college. President de Gaulle won convincingly at the June elections but, in light of the May riots, promised reform. A letter from Monsieur d'Espérey confirmed that Hilda had indeed pleaded not guilty to the charges against her. A second letter, the following month, asked me to appear in court on the twenty-first of October.

One Friday evening, we finished early. Rehearsals had gone well and I was pleased with how hard everyone had worked and allowed them home early to start the weekend. For me, however, work was never finished. I wrapped up some business and grabbed a bite to eat from the theatre restaurant.

An hour or so later, I decided to disappear to a local bar; less chance, I thought, of being disturbed. Although it was still only four o'clock, *Le Bar Rocco*, as it was called, was already quite busy, small groups of people chatting, elsewhere a couple held hands over the table top. The place was big with a large central area encircled by a number of booths. Gentle jazz and soft amber lighting added to the relaxed atmosphere. The staff were all young and good looking. I wondered how many of them had taken to the streets four months earlier. I sat down in a booth tucked away in a quieter corner and, having spread out my papers, ordered a beer. The issue that was taxing me at this point was the availability of a studio engineer I particularly valued. He was much in demand and my American bosses had seen fit to assign him to work on another, to my mind, minor project. I composed a letter, decided it wasn't persuasive enough, screwed it up and started again. I was nearing the end of my third attempt when a familiar voice said hello to me. Looking up, I was surprised to see Isabelle standing at the end of my table. I was taken aback by how delighted I was to see her. 'I won't disturb you,' she said. 'I can see you're busy. I just thought I'd say hello.'

'It's very nice of you. Are you here with… I'm sorry, I forget your boyfriend's name.' The image of Jesus flashed across my mind.

'Jacques. No, he's at college revising. He's got a big exam coming up. I'm here with my girlfriends,' she said, motioning behind with her head. Near the bar was a group of four fashionably-dressed girls of Isabelle's age, leaning in towards each other, all talking at the same time in high-pitched voices.

'So I see.'

'They're a bit loud, aren't they? I'll ask them to keep it down a bit.'

'No, don't do that. They're perfectly entitled to be as loud as they want. If I wanted peace and quiet, I would have gone to a library.'

She laughed. 'I'd better get back.'

'Yes, of course. Have a lovely evening.'

I ordered a second beer and tried to focus on my letter but instead I kept glancing up at the girls. How I envied them – to be young, in the capital and living in such prosperous times. When I was their age, we were still an occupied country, our lives restricted by the lack of opportunity and blighted by boredom. They were all attractive in their own way, attractive by the mere dint of being young. I eyed Isabelle, seeing her outside the orchestral environment for the first time, being herself. She was a person who spoke with her hands, gesticulating wildly, emphasising her point. I knew then how attracted I was to her. I had been from the moment I first saw her at the interview but then I was still a man who yearned for the love of his wife. I realised then, in that bar, with Isabelle and her friends nearby, that I felt lonely. I had a wife, so many friends, and was adored by the multitudes, and yet... I had no one. Being a conductor is, ultimately, a lonely job – you are the boss and the musicians treat you as such; polite, respectful but always at a distance. I knew too that I had somehow been weakened, unwittingly, by Hilda. She existed in my mind as two people – the woman I'd met twenty years ago and the person I knew today. I felt, somehow, sullied by my association with her younger self while, at the same time, deeply sorry for the woman she was now. Her downfall had left me feeling vulnerable. For the first time in my life, I felt sorry for myself.

An hour passed.

'Maestro, you look like you have the world on your shoulders.'

'My word.'

'I'm sorry, I didn't mean to make you jump.'

'It's fine. What happened to your friends?'

'They had to go. I was about to leave but I thought…'

'Well, join me.'

'I wouldn't want—'

'No, do. I'm bored of being on my own.'

She glanced behind her, as if ensuring her friends had left, then, with a little shrug of the shoulders, slid onto the bench beside me.

'I'll get you a glass of wine.'

'I shouldn't; I've had too many already.'

'Come now, one more won't hurt.'

And so we talked for two, maybe three hours. The bar became steadily busier and louder, and after a while we had to raise our voices to hear each other. A group of drinkers asked if they could share our table which, for me, seemed like a good time to call it a day. Isabelle escorted me as I returned to my office in the theatre from where I phoned through for a car.

Sliding open the glass partition, I ordered the driver to

70

take me home via Isabelle's. We sat in the back, Isabelle grinning and stroking the leather seats. 'I'm not used to such luxury,' she purred.

'Let's call it a perk of the job.'

We talked some more as the car meandered its way through the streets of Paris and out into the suburbs. The car smelt of leather and Isabelle's perfume. I enjoyed her company and, for the first time in an age, found myself laughing.

'We're here already,' said Isabelle as the car slowed down. 'That was quick. It's just at the end of this road.'

I told the driver where to stop.

'Well, thank you, Maestro,' she said, buttoning up her coat. 'It's been a lovely evening.' I couldn't see her expression in the dark but her tone sounded sincere.

'Yes,' I said, 'we must do it again some time.'

'Maestro, would you like, I mean, if you have time; what I want to say is…'

'Are you inviting me in for a cup of coffee?'

'I wouldn't want to speak out of turn.'

I leant over and kissed her hard, taking her, and myself, by surprise.

'Oh,' she breathed. 'I'll take that as a yes.'

'I'm sorry,' I said, biting my fist. 'I don't know what… I'm really sorry–'

She took my hand from my mouth, stroking it. 'Shush now, it's fine, it's OK. Come and have a coffee.'

'Won't your boyfriend be in?'

'We don't live together.'

'I'll tell the driver to wait.'

A street lamp illuminated her eyes. Hesitantly, she said, 'Send him home.' She smiled.

The car came to a halt. I saw the driver's eyes in the rear view mirror. Leaving the engine on, he darted out and opened the door for her. I followed her out, telling myself that I mustn't give in, that I had to resist. But she doesn't love you, I told myself, never had, never will. I felt the anger rise within me, a tightening in my chest. So why the hell did she marry me, then? Why the pretence all these years? I gave the driver a few francs as a tip. 'Thank you,' I said. 'You can call it a day now.'

Involuntarily, he shot a look at Isabelle who had wandered off to wait from a discreet distance. He nodded. 'Thank you, Monsieur.'

'Come,' she said, as the car drove off, an intense look in her eyes. 'Let's go up.' She took my hand. After just a few steps, I stopped and glanced back to see the tail lights of the car recede into the distance. 'Are you OK?'

'Yes,' I said. 'I'm fine.'

She lived in a small apartment on the fourth floor of a fine Art Nouveau block with ironwork balconies. She unlocked the door and pulled me in. Slamming the door shut behind me, she pushed me against it and kissed me with an urgency I'd never experienced before, her cold hands pulling my shirt free of my trousers. Ripping off our coats, she led me to her bedroom, her lips never leaving mine. By the time we got to her bed we were already half undressed, a trail of discarded clothes and shoes, hers and mine, littering the floor. She threw me onto her bed and reached over and switched on her bedside lamp. Straddling me, grinning in anticipation, she removed her bra.

*

Afterwards, I lay on my back, catching my breath, and felt a deep sense of contentment. She lay on her front, nestling into my neck; her arm drooped across my chest. 'Well, Maestro, that was quite something.' I felt the warmth of her breath against my skin. 'I bet you sleep with all your female musicians.'

'No, not at all!'

'Ha! I don't believe you.'

'No, really. You're the first.'

'Anyway, I don't mind. You're very good for an older

man.'

I laughed at another backhanded compliment. 'If you could just pass me my walking stick?'

She thumped me playfully on my chest. 'What about your wife? Won't she be missing you?'

'You know I'm married?'

'Of course. You wear a ring.'

I held up my hand, inspecting my wedding ring and sighed. 'No, she won't miss me at all.' If she did, I thought, I wouldn't now be in this situation.

She fell asleep lying next to me while I took in my surroundings – its high ceiling, striped blue wallpaper, a large dresser adorned with make-up and jewellery boxes, a framed Picasso print and, in the corner, a cello case. It was, I felt, a room full of love and warmth, perfectly reflecting my pretty young cellist. Resting my hand on her back, feeling the defined outline of her ribcage, I looked down at her, this delicate little thing, the wisps of hair covering her face, her arched, finely-plucked eyebrows, her flawless skin, this vulnerable, beautiful girl, and I had to swallow back my tears.

*

We awoke the following morning, a Saturday, and made love again with the autumnal sunshine streaming through her curtains, the constant hum of city traffic from below.

'What are your plans today?' I asked, as finally, having showered and dressed, we ate a breakfast of boiled eggs and toast and strong coffee in her living room. The radio played English pop music in the background.

'Jacques and I are going to the new Kandinsky exhibition at the Louvre.' I tried not to wince on hearing the name of her boyfriend.

'Is he one of those painters that produces mishmashes of shapes and colour?'

'It's lovely, so vibrant.'

'Yes.' I thought it best, at this point, not to reveal what I thought of this type of art, that is, if one can call it art.

'And you, Maestro; what are your plans?'

'Huh, I'll do what I do every Saturday – I shall lock myself away in my study and work.'

'All you do is work,' she said, dipping a piece of toast into her egg. 'You must give yourself a day off sometime.'

'I know, you're right.' Yet, I thought, working was the only way to keep out of Michèle's way.

A large fireplace dominated the room, candleholders on the mantelpiece, a gold-framed octagonal mirror above it; in the centre of the room a low oval table piled high with fashion magazines and, to the side, a copy of *Le Monde*.

'What's this song?' I asked on hearing something on the radio I hadn't heard before.

'Oh, it's good this, isn't it? It's *All or Nothing* by a band called The Small Faces,' she said, pronouncing the names in an exaggerated English accent.

'Very good, Isabelle, you'd make a good English disc jockey.'

She laughed. 'Thank you kindly, Monsieur Conductor.'

The song finished. Another started. 'Ah, now I know this one.'

'Of course, we all do. How could you not?'

It was The Beatles' *Hey Jude*. I thought of Hilda and her dismissive opinion on the Fab Four.

With a sudden movement of her hands, Isabelle knocked over the saltcellar. 'Silly me,' she said.

'I didn't know there was a new Kandinsky exhibition.'

'Yes, it's got of a good review in *Le Monde*,' she said, pointing to the newspaper. 'Did you read the paper yesterday?'

'No, I never get the time,' I said, scraping out the last of the egg.

'So you wouldn't have read about this case coming up with that woman from the war?' she asked, wiping crumbs from her fingers.

I stirred in an extra spoonful of sugar into my coffee.

'What woman?'

'She's only just been found. She was a guard at Drancy, you know?'

I spluttered on my coffee.

'Are you alright?'

'Yes, yes,' I said, thumping my chest. 'Drancy, the concentration camp?'

'Yeah. A right bitch, by the sounds of it, working for the Nazis – doing their dirty work.' She picked up her coffee bowl. 'I hope she pays for it.'

'Careful, Isabelle, we have no right to pre-judge.'

Slowly, she placed the bowl on the table. 'I can,' she said in a flat voice. Her eyes changed, their brightness dissolving into something altogether darker.

'What do you mean?'

She held her breath and cast her eyes down at the tablecloth. 'My father was sent to Drancy. He was on one of the last transports out of there to Auschwitz.'

'Oh.' I wasn't sure how to proceed.

'I'm Jewish.'

'I see. I didn't know.'

She pulled a face. 'So what? Does it change anything?'

'No, of course not.'

We sat in silence for a while. I wanted to ask whether her

father had survived. Instead, I watched her as she made a circle of salt with her fingertip. 'I'm twenty-three; born at the end of 1944. I never met my father.'

'I'm—'

'My parents were hiding out in a village up in the hills above Lyon. They were staying with good people, a whole community of farmers who wanted to protect the Jews. But it was getting more difficult. Twice, the Germans had come on searches, offering rewards to those prepared to denounce the Jews. My parents got away with it but they knew it'd be only a matter of time. And then Maman fell pregnant with me. This would have been in the last few months of the occupation, spring forty-four. They decided they had to do something before she became too, I don't know, incapacitated. They tried to get over the border into Switzerland. Lots of people had already gone that way. But someone denounced them, and they were arrested and sent to Drancy, where they were separated. They were kept in inhumane conditions, and beaten for no reason. The article says the camp was run by the Nazis. The French ran it at first until the Germans took over but they don't mention that. Too ashamed, I suppose. Maman never saw Papa again. He was put on a train to Auschwitz, that much she knew. She was kept in Drancy. She always thought she'd lose me; they were all so undernourished. But she survived, and I too, as you can see, survived. I was born terribly premature. Explains, I guess, why I've always been so skinny.'

'You're perfect, Isabelle.'

She smiled and reached for my hand across the table.

'You're too kind, Maestro. So you see, no one who worked at Drancy can be innocent.' She rose from the table and fetched the newspaper. Flicking through the pages, she found the article. 'Here it is. Her name's Hilda Lapointe. Look at her, she looks like a right monster, don't you think?'

She passed the paper over the table. My mouth went dry on seeing her police mug shot. I was shocked by the intense coldness of her eyes, her thin lips, the solid outline of her jaw. Isabelle was right – she did look like a monster.

I read the opening paragraph:

She has escaped justice for over two decades, but next month, at Le Palais de Justice, *68-year-old Hilda Lapointe, a former guard at the wartime internment camp in the Parisian suburb of Drancy, will finally come face-to-face with her accusers. Nicknamed 'The Lady with the Truncheon' by her victims, she was infamous for wielding her club against the Jewish inmates at this Nazi-run camp.*

Unable to read any more, I folded the paper and placed it neatly on the table.

'Are you OK, Maestro? You look worried about something.'

'No, I'm fine. Just fine,' I said quietly.

*

I spent the afternoon locked in my study, brooding. The article in *Le Monde* had deeply shocked me. I had no idea Hilda's case would attract any attention at all, let alone the attention of a national newspaper. When Monsieur d'Espérey had asked me to speak on Hilda's behalf, I had no perception whatsoever that people and the media might be interested. I rang the lawyer straightaway.

'What did you expect, Maestro? Of course something like this would cause interest.'

'But it was the war, for God's sake, twenty-three years ago. Haven't people moved on?'

He laughed but not in a way that implied he'd found anything funny. 'Twenty-three years is not so very long, Maestro. You, Monsieur, conduct music hundreds of years old so surely you must appreciate that.'

'I just didn't think... I didn't realise... Oh, it doesn't matter. Anyway, my point is, I don't think I can help you any more.'

'Meaning...?'

'I mean...' He knew damn well what I meant – he merely wanted to make it difficult for me. 'Mademoiselle Lapointe, I can't…. Damn it, man, I've got my reputation to think of.'

Immediately, I regretted using the phrase and he picked up on it. 'Your reputation, Maestro?'

'The woman worked in France's most notorious concentration camp, you said yourself that she was guilty of… war crimes, didn't you say? I'm well known, you know that, I can't be seen condoning the actions of some sadistic camp guard.'

'Our case lies on the fact she was coerced to act the way she did, both by her masters and the environment, that she was an unwilling accomplice. Look, she is a woman who's always kept herself to herself. She has no friends, no family. She is alone in the world, alone and very much afraid. If you can stand up for her and say, look, she may have been bad but she wasn't all bad, it will help us prove that, at core, she was a good woman led astray by circumstances. We can't do it without you, Maestro.'

'What about her friend, the one she lived with in Saint-Romain after the war.'

'Yes, I know. Alas, she died.'

'Oh.'

'Yes, exactly. She has you and no one else. You know, she's hinted at… at doing away with herself. Those were her words.'

'Really?' Well, I thought, that would solve everything. 'Do you think she would?'

'No. She was a bully, and we all know bullies are, essentially, cowards.'

I didn't know what to say. Picking up on my silence, the lawyer continued. 'Naturally, it's your choice but this reputation you mention, and I do understand, was built on the fact you survived the war. And I'm sure you'd agree with me that your survival was in no small part secured by the woman who now depends on you. But, as I say, it's all your own choice, Maestro.'

*

My conversation with Hilda's lawyer had left me in a constant state of anxiety. People had been sent to their deaths from Drancy; people had died there. I thought of Isabelle's parents. Who knows, perhaps the paths of Hilda and Isabelle's parents had crossed. What was Hilda's role at Drancy; to what extent was she guilty of terrible things? Perhaps she was no more than a scapegoat, like she'd said.

We worked hard on rehearsing the Berlioz and a couple of supplementary pieces but, for the first time in my life, I had difficulty applying myself. I even had difficulty getting up in the morning. I missed my wife. We had always led separate lives but now, after her announcement, I felt as if I was sharing a house with a stranger. Morocco seemed like a long time ago. Meanwhile, every day at work, I had to see Isabelle, a member of my team, awaiting my instruction. I felt self-conscious in front of her – and went out of my way to not over praise or criticise her, convinced that others would see through our body language. Yet, I certainly did not regret having her as my mistress – not now. After that first day, I returned and slept the night a second time soon afterwards. I found Isabelle a delight to be with; I loved her company. She was witty and intelligent, and could hold her own in any discussion. And she was still a valued member of my orchestra.

The fact that we were both being unfaithful caused her, I think, no concern – until one Sunday afternoon. We were lounging on her settee, warm with the afterglow of sex, reading the papers, listening to the radio, the sort of things I had always envisioned doing with Michèle – just *being* together, silently enjoying each other's company, when her doorbell rang. She sprang up from the settee, swearing. 'It's Jacques,' she shrieked.

'How do you know?'

'He has a special ring. Christ, put your shoes on. Shit, what do we do?'

'You're not going to make me stand on the balcony, are

you?'

'You've come over because of work,' she said, knowing I never went anywhere without a work file in my briefcase. 'Turn the radio off,' she said as, quickly, she tidied up the magazines and newspapers. She leapt over to the intercom, still buttoning up her blouse and straightening her hair, and pressed the button to allow her boyfriend up.

By the time he walked across the foyer, called for the lift, went up to the fourth floor and walked down the corridor, Isabelle and I were sitting at the table, with paper and sheet music scattered round, looking the part. She welcomed him in with a lingering hug and a sloppy kiss while I averted my eyes and tried to sit on my jealousy. We shook hands as she re-introduced us. He grimaced in an attempt at a smile and I knew he suspected that something was amiss. I had to make my excuses and leave as soon as I could.

It was only as I was putting on my coat I realised I'd left my tie in Isabelle's bedroom. I could not think of a single plausible reason why I should need to go into there, and unless Jacques went to use Isabelle's toilet, I wouldn't be able to speak to her alone. I had no choice – I would simply have to leave and hope to God that if they did decide to go to bed, that it would be Isabelle and not Jacques who found my tie of many colours. The thought of Isabelle taking Jacques to her still-warm bed left me feeling quite nauseous.

I caught the Métro home. Catching the Métro had become part of my daily routine now, allowing me to connect to real people. I had come to realise that I was too closeted from the world – from home to the theatre, and from the theatre back to home, in a luxury car with its own driver. The journey allowed me too much time to think, to dwell on problems that offered nothing by the way of solution. In the confines of the car, I felt suffocated by thoughts of Hilda, of knowing what had happened to Isabelle's parents. The Métro with its anonymity and all its passengers allowed me an escape which even music could no longer provide.

*

Seeing Isabelle at rehearsals was wonderfully tortuous – my heart would surge upon seeing her and as much as I wanted to sneakily take her to one side and kiss her, I knew I couldn't. I could tell the other men in the orchestra found her attractive as well but, I thought gleefully to myself, she's mine!

We were having a break, and I stepped out onto the patio for some fresh air. Autumn was well on its way, one could feel it in the air. Groups of my musicians congregated. It's always amused me how musicians stick to their own – the woodwind players in this corner, the percussion in that. Isabelle was out there with some of her string players, laughing, twiddling with a bow in her hair. She looked beautiful in a knee-length dress with a lace hem, her thin legs and her freckled arms dangling with bracelets. I was desperate for her to come talk to me. Instead, I watched her with her colleagues, laughing, young, so full of life. I ached with desire yet, at that moment, observing her, I knew it would never last.

People nodded at me but I remained, as always, alone. No one, unless they want something, wants to speak to the boss. Power places one on a lonely pedestal.

I turned my back to view the city below, the avenues disappearing into the distance, the hum of traffic, the vibrant, living city. I gripped the balcony and realised how much I missed my wife. Isabelle was beautiful but I knew, given the choice, I wanted Michèle back. We'd drifted so far apart, we'd become strangers to each other. But when, when I looked back on our time together, I realised there'd always been this distance between us, she'd lived her life behind a protective shield and no one, not even her husband, was allowed anywhere near. I often wondered what she'd been like before the Gestapo had tortured her. Her parents had died before I met her, I knew no one from her life before me. Looking up at the clouds, I realised I had tears rolling down my cheeks.

*

Hilda's trial was due to start on the Monday and was expected to last most of the week. I had been scheduled to appear on the Wednesday. The recorded concert was due to take place the following Saturday. I asked Michèle whether she'd like to attend the concert. No, she said, she had other plans. I tried not to show my disappointment – it'd been years since she'd come watch me perform. Her lack of interest had always hurt, but never as much as now. But, oddly enough, she suggested I go see a dentist ahead of the performance, saying that my teeth needed a professional clean. But I'll have my back to the audience, I said. No one will see my teeth, apart from the orchestra, and they've seen them many times before. She insisted; she knew of a dentist who could whiten them up for me.

We should have been rehearsing every day in the lead up to such a momentous performance but, in order to attend court, I had given the orchestra the whole of Wednesday off. I didn't tell them why, and I certainly didn't tell Isabelle. It felt like a dirty secret. I knew I had to tell her at some point – after all, she'd find out soon enough, what with the media waiting on the sidelines, sharpening their knives.

Monday came and went. I knew Tuesday's papers would

carry a report from the first day of the case but I chose not to buy a copy. I felt worried enough as it was without having my confidence, or lack of it, undermined any further. The rehearsals were a painful affair, my concentration now shot at, not by Isabelle's presence, but by this black cloud that followed my every step.

On Tuesday evening, after work, Isabelle and I retired to *Le Bar Rocco*. It was still early, the music quiet and the place largely deserted. We sat in the same booth as before and ate a mediocre meal and drank passable wine. She seemed subdued, as subdued as I felt. We barely talked, although I did ask her whether she thought my teeth needed whitening. Eventually, as we were finishing our desserts, she said quietly, 'He found your tie, you know.'

My spoonful of crème caramel stopped half way to my mouth. 'Oh.'

'Yes.'

'What did you say?'

She almost laughed as she told me. 'I came up with the most ridiculous of excuses. I said you'd spilt coffee down it earlier in the day and I said I'd wash it for you, and just threw it in the bedroom until later.'

'That's terrible.'

'And what would you have said off the cuff that would

have been any better?' She wasn't laughing now.

'You're right. I'm sorry.' After a long pause, during which I contemplated my dessert, I asked, 'Did he believe you?'

'He pretended to.'

We didn't speak for a few minutes as we struggled through the rest of our desserts. I asked whether I should call for the bill.

She didn't answer. Instead she said quietly, 'I'm going to court tomorrow, for that case we read about in the papers. The guard at Drancy.'

I felt my face redden. I had to dissuade her. 'But why, Isabelle?' I reached for her hand. 'It'll make it worse for you.'

'I have to know. I need to know what went on there. If I had time, I'd go every day.'

'Would your mother thank you for it?'

'She won't know.'

'It's not for me to say, Isabelle, but… I don't think it's a good idea.'

'You're right.' I enjoyed a moment of optimism until she looked straight at me. 'It's not for you to say.'

I got the bill.

*

I returned home. If I was worried about appearing in court before, now I was panicked. I found Michèle watching TV. I poured myself a beer and slumped on the settee next to her and pretended to take an interest in a documentary about President Kennedy. I wanted to tell her everything, she was still my wife after all, but the words wouldn't come. I wondered how we'd become so estranged. Hadn't I given her everything? I looked round our living room in all its glory – the leather three-piece suite, the Turkish rugs, the chandelier, our own cocktail cabinet, despite my preference for beer, the gold-framed mirror, the yucca plant. Upon the mantelpiece, various souvenirs from Morocco, including a decorative tagine and a brightly-coloured teapot with a long, curved spout. God, how ostentatious it looked, and how, all of a sudden, I hated it. I wondered whether she too had seen Hilda's story in the papers. After all, she had also suffered at the hands of the Nazis. Our lack of children was the result, her inability to love me another. The documentary came to an end. She shuffled to the kitchen to make her cocoa and fill a hot water bottle, despite it still being warm, and we retired to our separate bedrooms.

Lying in bed, I picked up the telephone. I had to tell Isabelle the truth. Better now, I thought, than she found me in court, standing up for the woman who represented those responsible for her parent's maltreatment and her father's death. She answered on the second ring. 'Jacques?' she said.

Swallowing my disappointment, I said hello. 'I... I wanted to make sure you were OK.'

'Of course.' She yawned and I couldn't help but wonder whether she would have done so had it been Jacques at the end of the line. 'Why wouldn't I be?'

'It's just... well, you seemed a bit quiet tonight, a bit pensive.'

'I'm worried, that's all, about tomorrow. It's a big thing for me, this court case. I'm nervous about how it might affect me, you know?'

'Yes.' It had to be now. 'Listen, Isabelle, about tomorrow—'

'I know, I'm just being silly. Ignore me; it'll be fine. Look, it's good of you to call, but I'm really tired. I have to go now. I'll see you on Thursday, Maestro.'

'But, Isabelle, wait...'

She'd hung up. I held the receiver for a while, its buzzing noise permeating my brain until, in a fit of frustration, I slammed it back into its cradle.

Paris, October 1968

Monsieur d'Espérey wasn't expecting me until the afternoon session. I got myself ready and, in my haste, cut myself shaving. Never had I felt in such a state of anxiety. Even the biggest and grandest of concerts hadn't reduced me to such a wreck. I deliberated over what to wear and finally opted for all black – as if going to a funeral. For a dash of colour, I added a fake carnation to my lapel then, deciding it inappropriate, removed it. Even Michèle, who never took an interest in my comings and goings, commented on my suit. A meeting with the record label bosses, I told her. She too was off out for the day and we made an elaborate dance of ensuring we didn't leave together.

Le Palais de Justice, a grand grey-stoned building in central Paris, is a spectacular if intimidating place. I'd heard that Marie Antoinette had been imprisoned here before being executed. I made my way to the chambers, as instructed, and there, sitting on a bench in the corridor, waited for Monsieur d'Espérey and Hilda. Finally, they appeared, following a break, and, for only the fourth time in my life, I met Hilda. She looked drawn and pale, her lips the same colour as her skin, but determined, having the air of someone ready to do battle. I spoke to them politely but couldn't bring myself to act friendly. I wanted them to know I was doing this under sufferance. She looked smart for the occasion – a matching deep-brown jacket and skirt, a collared shirt with a black necktie. She shook my hand firmly. 'I can't thank you enough,' she said.

'What's the matter with your face,' asked Monsieur d'Espérey.

'What? Oh, I cut myself shaving. So, how's it been going?'

He glanced at Hilda. 'Not too well, if I'm honest.' He removed his wig and, inspecting the inside, said, 'The prosecution have chosen their witnesses well – they're all articulate, have good memories, and they each hold a deep-rooted hatred for Hilda here.'

I had to stop myself from saying, "what did you expect?" Instead, I asked, 'Am I next then?'

'No, they're running behind time. They have one more to go. I fear they've saved their best for last.' Giving his wig a shake, he continued, 'All the more reason why you must play your part, Maestro. You and the others.'

'Others? I thought–'

'We managed to dredge up a couple of Hilda's former pupils.'

'Pupils?'

'I used to be a teacher,' said Hilda, with a wry smile. 'Music.'

'You were a music teacher?'

She pulled a face. 'Before the war. At a Catholic girls' school. Did I not mention it?'

'No. No, you never mentioned it. I think I would've remembered.'

'Well, we all have a few surprises, don't we?'

*

'Madame Kahn, how old were you at the time of your arrest?'

'I was fifteen.'

'Why were you arrested?'

She shrugged as if it was a silly question. 'Because I'm Jewish.'

'And when was this?'

'Fourth December 1943.' A thin woman with sunken cheeks, Madame Kahn pulled on the beads around her neck.

'Were any other members of your family arrested at the same time?'

'Yes, my parents, my grandmother and my younger sister.'

'What happened to them?'

'Suzanne, my sister, and I were separated from our parents and—'

'Forcibly?'

'Yes. It was… horrible. We tried to cling onto them. Suzanne became hysterical, well, we all did. There were hundreds of families like us, all being pulled apart. They kicked us and beat us with their sticks, and used water hoses against us. The noise, the screaming, will live with me forever. That's when I first remember seeing her.'

'Her? The accused?'

She pointed at Hilda, who sat impassively, without expression. 'Yes, her.'

'Irène d'Urville or, as she is known today, Hilda Lapointe.'

I glanced around at my surroundings. The courtroom lacked the style of its exterior. A plain wall-to-wall brown carpet and wood-panelled walls made it all seem rather bleak. The public sat either on a raised platform behind or in a gallery above. Every space was taken. Without wanting to make it too obvious, I searched for Isabelle but couldn't see her. Perhaps she hadn't come after all. On the walls, various framed portraits of serious-looking men in wigs, while behind the judge, a larger portrait of President de Gaulle with his long

95

nose, his knowing eyes and slightly-contemptuous stare. To one side sat the twelve men and women of the jury. The judge, a gaunt man with thick glasses on the end of a thin nose, listened intently as the prosecutor asked Madame Kahn his next question.

'Now, could you tell the court what Madame d'Urville was doing at the point you first arrived at Drancy?'

'Shouting and ordering her staff around.'

'Did you see her use force?'

'No, but others were on her orders.'

He paused a moment to look at his notes. 'Did you see your family again?'

'Suzanne and I were kept together. I never saw my mother or father again, or grandma.'

'What happened to them?'

'At the time I didn't know but after the war I learnt they'd been deported to Auschwitz.'

'And…?'

She bowed her head and muttered, 'They were gassed.'

'All three of them?'

'Yes.'

'Did your sister survive?

'Yes but she…'

He lowered his eyes at her. 'Go on.'

'She took her own life – five years ago.'

'I see.'

She looked to the floor and quietly produced a handkerchief which she held tightly in her hand. He allowed her a few moments to compose herself. 'Madame Kahn, how long were you incarcerated at Drancy?'

'Eight months.'

'Could you please describe for the court the conditions there?'

'Yes. It was terribly overcrowded. I found out after the war that the place was designed for 700 people yet there were 7,000 of us crammed into there at any one time. We slept fifty to a dorm. The lucky ones had bunk beds or even just planks to sleep on. Others slept on straw on the floor. We were fed abysmally – watery soup that tasted like soap, no protein. People died of malnourishment. There was hardly any fresh water and only two toilets.'

'Two toilets for 7,000 inmates?'

'Yes, you can imagine what it was like. People fell ill all the time and many of them died. There was little electricity so during winter we were always very cold, shivering constantly.'

'Was the security tight?'

'Of course. There was barbed wire everywhere, searchlights, watchtowers, and men with machine guns. As

Jews, we weren't allowed to look at any German or French guard in the eye. If we met a guard, say, on the staircase, we had to stop and push ourselves flat against the wall.'

'And during these eight months, did you have much contact with the accused?'

'We saw her almost everyday. Some of the guards were OK, some were nasty only occasionally, as if it was expected of them, but she was the worst. We were all very frightened of her.'

'In what way exactly?'

'Well, if… I mean, whenever you saw her, you were on tenterhooks in case she lashed out at you.'

'Perhaps you gave her reason to?'

'No, not at all. She…' The woman turned to face Hilda. 'She didn't need a reason.'

'Could you tell the court the reasons for your fear?'

'She carried a truncheon and she used it all the time, whether you deserved it or not. Everyone called her "the lady with the truncheon".'

The judge spoke, 'Did you say a truncheon?'

'Yes, it was a wooden one with a leather strap.'

'I see. Carry on.'

The prosecutor cleared his throat. 'Madame Kahn, could you describe what happened one morning in early February of

1944?'

'Yes. Every morning we had to line up for roll call. We had to stand there, in lines of five, absolutely still, usually for about two hours, whatever the weather. It might not sound much but when you're starving hungry and weak, possibly ill, and cold and frightened, then I can't describe how difficult it is.'

'Do continue.'

'On this particular morning in February, Madame d'Urville said that someone had stolen food from the kitchens. No one admitted to it. Probably because it didn't happen–'

'But you can't be sure of this fact?'

'No. We were starving, like I said, so it could've happened.'

'What did she do?'

'She… she made us undress. All of us.'

'Down to your underwear?'

'No.' She cast her eyes downwards. 'Naked.'

'It was cold?'

'Yes, it was snowing and there was ice on the ground. It was February after all. We had to remain totally still. If anyone moved, Madame d'Urville would hit us with her truncheon.'

'On what part of the body did she hit you?'

'Usually, across the breasts.'

He raised his eyebrows. 'Carry on.'

'She would walk up and down in her thick coat and boots, watching us like a wolf, while we stood there humiliated in our nakedness. Every half an hour or so, she returned to the staff quarters to warm up for a few minutes and some other woman would come to take her place.'

'Do you remember this other woman's name?'

'No.'

'Did this other woman hit you?'

'No, in fact she even allowed us to wrap our arms round ourselves. We were all shivering like crazy. But with Madame d'Urville we had to stand with our arms at our sides. Many of the girls started crying. The girl next to me lost control of her bladder. I remember trying to step in her urine just to warm up the soles of my feet. Another one became hysterical.'

'What happened to this woman?'

Madame Kahn glanced from the lawyer to Hilda and back again. 'She slapped her across the face then hit her several times until she fell. I mean, she hit her really hard with her club. Then she carried on hitting her across the... the backside and over her head, everywhere, and kicking her. The woman curled up in a ball on the ice, all naked. I remember the sound of her boots cracking her ribcage. She, Madame d'Urville, lost control; she looked like something possessed. She hit that poor woman until blood poured from her mouth and ears. Then, suddenly, it stopped, and Madame d'Urville looked, I don't know, exhilarated.' She closed her eyes. 'Madame d'Urville ordered two of us to take her to the infirmary.'

'You were one of them.'

'Yes, me and the girl who had peed herself, about my age. I took the woman by the legs and the other girl by the arms. She was covered in blood and some of her bones...'

'Yes?'

'Some of her bones were sticking out at odd angles.'

'I see.'

'Although she was rake thin, so were we, and we hardly had the strength to lift her and we were blue with cold. I remember...'

'Yes?'

She sighed. 'Once we were out of Madame d'Urville's vision, we put her on the ground so we could catch our breaths. We felt awful, just leaving her heaped on the ground like that, like a sack of potatoes, naked and all bloodied. We embraced each other, really tightly, to try and warm up a bit. We were both crying and our teeth were chattering. We took her to the infirmary and even they felt sorry for us, and gave us a blanket each.'

Speaking slowly, the lawyer asked, 'Did you know the

woman you carried?'

'I had spoken to her but I didn't know her name. She wasn't young; perhaps about forty. But it's difficult to tell a person's age when they're almost dead from starvation.'

'Do you know what happened to this woman?'

'I heard she died a few days later.'

'As a result of the beating?'

She cast her eyes at the judge. 'I wouldn't know that for sure, but it couldn't have helped.'

The lawyer nodded knowingly. 'Thank you, Madame Kahn. No more questions.'

The judge looked at Monsieur d'Espérey who shook his head. He had nothing to ask.

The judge called for a brief adjournment.

*

I spent a few minutes in the lavatory, staring at myself in the mirror. Madame Kahn's story was upsetting, naturally, and now I was expected to stand in front of a packed courtroom, full of reporters, and tell the world that Irène d'Urville wasn't such a bad sort. I had a headache, I felt nauseous, my mouth felt dry. What had brought me to this place? If I'd known, all those years ago, that I'd now be in this situation, I think I would have taken my chances with the Gestapo. I combed my hair and took a gulp of water. But still, I felt sick.

Leaving the lavatory, I bumped straight into Isabelle. We stood in the corridor, simply staring at each other. She too had dressed up for the occasion, wearing a slim-lined grey skirt and a matching jacket, her hair pulled back. Eventually, she asked what was I doing there. 'Just been to the toilet,' I said, hoping to inject a lighter note.

'You've come to support me,' she said, with the faintest of smiles. 'Jacques is here though. You look very smart for the occasion.'

'I'm a character witness for the accused.' There, at last, I'd said it.

She tilted her head, as if better to understand. 'What did you say?'

'It's a long story but—'

'You're a character witness? For *her* – that bitch in there?'

A couple of court clerks passed by, laughing. I watched them as they made their way down the corridor. 'I'm sorry.'

'I... I don't understand. Do you *actually* know her?'

'Well, not really. It was during the war. I, erm...'

'No, wait; let me get this straight. You are about to go in there and say something nice about the woman who worked for the regime that killed my father? Is that right? Because if it is...'

103

'Isabelle.' I reached out for her but she stepped back.

'So it's true – that's what you're doing here.' She looked at me with utter contempt and I felt myself diminish under her hateful gaze.

I was almost tearful as I croaked, 'I have no choice—'

'No choice?' She spat out the words. 'My parents had no choice; Madame Kahn in there had no choice, but you do. You have a choice.'

D'Espérey appeared. With a quick nod, he said a curt hello to Isabelle. 'Maestro, we've been called back in.'

'I'm sorry, Isabelle.' I followed the lawyer back into the courtroom.

*

'You are well known, Monsieur; a conductor of some repute,' said d'Espérey, his thumbs hooked into his waistcoat.

'I like to think so.'

'Could you speak up?' said the judge.

'I'm sorry, Your Honour. I said I'd like to think so.'

He asked me to relate my background story – my age, where I was brought up, my interest in music, my training. I spoke at length, hoping to come across as a decent human being, hoping to delay the inevitable. Then it came to my activities during the war, I confessed I was little more than a messenger but I embellished the importance of what was within those missives, how the information I delivered on a 'regular basis' had provided the necessary means of communication in order to launch attacks against the German occupiers. Lucky, I thought, that my man in the village had been executed. I wondered what had happened to the train guard from Africa. I emphasised how I had to use my cunning to pass by the Germans without ever rousing their suspicion. 'On one occasion,' I told them, 'I had to rush to the train toilet in order to escape them. When they knocked on the door, I had no option but to rip up the paper and throw it out of the window. They searched me and found nothing.' It was a complete lie. Looking up, I saw Isabelle, sitting towards the back of the courtroom, Jacques next to her.

'Quite the resistance hero then?'

'Well, I wouldn't go quite that far.' I hoped Isabelle was paying attention at this point.

'And it was in this capacity as a messenger for the resistance that you met the accused, Hilda Lapointe?'

'Yes, but only the once, and I didn't know her name.'

'Did you know where she worked?'

'No, not at all.' I glanced over at Hilda, who sat there, her eyes fixed on me.

'Could you tell the court about the occasion your paths

crossed?'

And so I told the court the story of that day in August 1942, 26 years previously. I started with a preamble about how a messenger, like me, had been arrested and tortured – I needed to emphasise the risk I was running. It felt strange – I was used to telling stories with music but here, for the first time, I was using words and I felt as if I had no control.

'She could quite easily have turned you in. From what you say, she suspected you, but she said nothing to the German guards.'

'Yes, I've thought about it many times since.'

'But she didn't,' he said loudly, turning to the jurors. 'She did not hand him over to the Germans.' Stroking his chin, Monsieur d'Espérey considered his next question. 'Did she gain anything from intervening on your behalf?'

'Not that I know of.'

'Do you think it fair to say that without the accused's intervention that day, your life might have turned out very differently?'

'Objection!' shouted the prosecutor. 'The question is pure speculation.'

'Quite,' said the judge. 'Objection upheld. Monsieur d'Espérey, may I remind you that a court of law deals in facts, not "what-ifs".'

'Of course, Your Honour. I do apologise. Speculation it may be, but we know of many, many cases when young men, sometimes boys, were cruelly tortured by the Nazi occupiers and frequently executed, whether they provided information or not. We also know that earlier in the war, those arrested were usually imprisoned for a while and, except for the ringleaders, released. But by the summer of 1942, many more were being executed, often for the slightest transgressions. It is speculation, but my point is that my client knew that without her intervention, this young man, as he was then, would have been under very great danger of torture and possibly execution.'

When asked, I told the court how, after the war, Hilda had come to see me just the once, in 1966, and that was it. In other words, we were not acquaintances in any sense of the word. 'Yet, in that conversation, I am right in thinking that you acknowledged your debt to the accused?'

'Yes.'

'Thank you. No more questions.'

*

Next came the prosecutor. He paced up and down in front of me, hands behind his back, as if collecting his thoughts. 'You were here this morning, were you not, so you would have heard the testimony of Madame Kahn. All week, we've been hearing similar stories – of habitual beatings, cruelty and maltreatment at the hands of Hilda Lapointe. What did you make of it?'

'I thought… I thought it was appalling.'

'Hmm, interesting. Yet, you are still prepared to stand in a court of law to act as a character witness for the woman who is accused of such barbaric acts?'

A titter of voices rose from the public galleries. 'Only because she may have saved my life. I wasn't to know—'

'But you do now! You've known for months, unless you live a life of a hermit, which we all know you do not. Yet, despite this knowledge, you still agreed. You could have said no at any point. You can still say no right this instance!'

'They were only accusations.' Someone booed.

'Silence!' said the judge.

'Only accusations? No, not accusations – facts. Her defence here is not that she didn't commit these crimes, but that she was under orders. So, leaving aside the second point for a moment, these acts are things that actually happened.'

'I… I suppose because I felt I owed her.' People hissed at me. I felt their loathing for me.

'You *owed* her? So because you were the beneficiary of this one single act of kindness, you feel you have the right to dismiss all these scores of victims.' Turning to the jury, he said, 'I repeat what I said at the beginning of this trial – the number of victims and witnesses number over eighty. Under court instruction, we have asked only a sample to come here this week to give evidence.' He returned his attention to me. 'So, despite what we all know to be fact, do you still feel that you *owe* the accused?'

I stood there, opened mouthed, shaking. I could feel Isabelle's eyes bearing down on me; I thought of her parents, of her murdered father. I saw Madame Kahn, gently shaking her head, living every day of her life with the memory that her family had been gassed, of picking that poor woman up from the icy ground. I felt the whole world looking at me, despising me for what I'd become.

'Well, Monsieur, we await your answer.'

I looked at Hilda and I hated her. Why had she done it, why had she intervened? I remembered our conversation: *One day I will be a conductor / Oh, you will, will you? You sound very sure of yourself. I wish you the very best of luck.* My life had come full circle, yet here I was consumed with a visceral hatred I'd never experienced before. How could she have done those things? To those poor, abused people.

'A simple yes or no – do you still feel that you owe the accused?'

I felt myself tremble as quietly, so quietly, I answered, 'Yes.'

*

I don't remember leaving the witness stand or how people looked at me. But often, since, I've had dreams in which a thousand angry faces leer at me, pointing, hissing, frothing at the mouth, blood seeping from their ears. I see scratch marks against the brown wooden panels of the courtroom. I see the judge donning a black wig. I see Isabelle's father leading me away to somewhere unknown and dark. I see Monsieur d'Espérey writing the word 'reputation' with a quill pen. I see Mary Magdalene with her shaved head, the swastika emblazoned on her chest. I call for her and I reach out. She sees me and she turns his back on me.

It took me years to work out the meaning of those scratch marks until, one day, I came across a photograph of the inside of a gas chamber – its walls were covered in those very same scratch marks.

I know I rushed out of the courtroom and staggered down the deserted corridor, lurching from one side to the other, falling against the walls. I went to the lavatory and, locking the cubicle door, lent over the toilet and was sick. What had I done, I asked myself again and again, what had I done?

I didn't stay to hear Monsieur d'Espérey call in Hilda's former pupils from her girls' school, and I certainly didn't hang around to watch Hilda's turn in the witness box. I had seen enough; I'd repaid my debt and now I wanted nothing else to do with it. The woman could go to Hell and rot, for all I cared.

I returned home to an empty house. I fixed myself a stiff drink and fell into the settee. Michèle was often out now. She didn't tell me where she went to or who she was with and somehow, even though I was still her husband, I no longer felt as if I had the right to ask. We were still in separate beds. At first, I'd hoped that this would prove a temporary measure, that soon she realised she missed me and perhaps loved me after all, and invite me back to the marital bed. I knew now that that wasn't going to happen, that I would never again share a bed with my wife. I listened to the quiet sounds of the house, the wind outside, the odd creak and I never felt so alone. I got drunk, and eventually staggered to bed.

The following day I felt no better, in fact, because of the hangover, I felt worse. I was dreading having to face Isabelle. Surely, she would see that I had been put into an impossible situation; that, despite what the prosecutor had said, I had had no choice. I was last to arrive, and the whole orchestra were already at their places, tuning their instruments. The combined effect of eighty musical instruments being tuned at the same time made my head throb. Clasping my temples, I yelled at them to stop. A sea of bewildered eyes turned to face me. I searched for Isabelle and couldn't see her. I went to get myself a cup of tea, and the cacophony started afresh. I made sure I was away long enough to ensure that by the time I returned, they had finished.

'I can't see Isabelle,' I said to no one in particular.

A fellow cellist stood, a middle-aged woman whose work I always valued. 'Maestro, I'm afraid to say Isabelle's phoned in to say she's resigned from the orchestra.'

'What?' I yelled. 'But surely, she'll do the concert.'

The woman shook her head. 'With immediate effect,' she said.

'She can't do that – her contract… Did you speak to her?'

'No, it was the office. Someone just came in to pass the message on.'

I almost pulled a fistful of hair from my scalp. We were two days from the concert and she was leaving me in the lurch? And what about us, me and her? Did this mean we were finished? God, I hoped not; I liked her too much to lose her.

I turned to my first violinist and asked her to take over

from me while I went off to make some phone calls.

Settling myself in my office, I tried ringing her. She didn't answer; I hadn't expected her to. I rang the record company and, being put through to my agent, told him what had happened. His reaction was much the same as mine. 'Her contract explicitly states that she can't do this. We could take her to court over this.'

'Maybe, but the question is who can we bring in at this stage?' I said frantically. I suggested the name of France's leading cellist.

'Him? You're mad – he'll cost a fortune, more than all the others put together.'

'He's the only reliable alternative we have at this stage. I've worked with him before; he's the only cellist I can think of who could pull it off. What choice do we have?'

I heard him sigh. 'You're right; we have no bloody choice. OK, I'll get on it.'

'Thank you.'

'Listen, Maestro, before you go, have you seen today's papers?'

My heart sank; I knew what was coming next. I heard him rustle the newspaper. 'The headline reads, "Conductor Condones the Collaborator".' He laughed. 'I love the alliteration. I congratulate you, Maestro.'

'You do?'

'If you weren't famous enough already, then this ensures there won't be a Frenchman anywhere who doesn't know your name. This'll make marvellous publicity.'

I returned to the orchestra, and for the rest of the day, we struggled on – hardly the ideal preparation for such a big occasion.

On the way home, I couldn't help myself and bought a copy of *Le Figaro*. My agent was right – the report on Hilda's third day in court was damning of both her and myself. Her former pupils were not even mentioned. I may have helped the resistance out, the article said, but in sticking up for the guard, I was no better than a collaborator. Hilda Lapointe will be damned for all eternity, it said, and I will be condemned alongside her.

I found the house empty again. I tried phoning Isabelle again but still no answer. I made myself a basic meal and settled down for an evening of pointless television. Surely, I thought, Isabelle would come round at some point; she couldn't remain angry with me forever. I liked her so much; I couldn't bear the thought of not seeing her and taking her into my arms. Isabelle was everything I wanted in a woman – beautiful, funny, intelligent, and a talented musician. God, I missed her.

I went to bed and dreamt of making love to Isabelle.

*

It's one of the great joys in a conductor's life – the start of the concert. The orchestra is ready; the audience is seated and awaiting your appearance; silence descends, edged with anticipation; the lights are dimmed. It is now, as a conductor, one makes one's appearance beneath the spotlight. It's Saturday night and everything is ready. Our replacement cellist, costing a small fortune, has stepped into Isabelle's shoes, all the top brass from my American record label are present, together with an assortment of music reviewers and even a couple of politicians. Every ticket has sold out; I heard rumours of tickets being sold on the black market for four or five times their face value. It is the biggest musical occasion of the year. I am a professional and all thoughts of Hilda, Drancy and Isabelle have been banished from my mind. I confess, I have butterflies but I know that on picking up the baton that I shall live for the music and the music alone. I hover in the stage wings. The stage manager uses a walkie-talkie to communicate with the lighting guy. All is set. He gives me the thumbs up. It is time.

I step out onto the stage and wait for the applause to hit me. There is an inexplicable delay. Then, instead of applause,

I'm greeted with a slow handclap. I feel the panic rising within me. I can't tell what's happening out there – the glare of the spotlight blinds me. Someone even has the audacity to boo me. How dare they? Don't they know who I am? I pick up the baton from the music stand and I realise I am shaking. I try to breathe away my nerves, to call on my inner resources. But I am stumbling; I feel my confidence seep away like water down a drain. I face my orchestra; I can see their concerned faces. I daren't turn around. I just need to start and allow the music to do the talking for me.

Two gruelling hours later, and we finish. I am sweating from every pore; I have never put so much effort into conducting and I am trembling with exhaustion. The audience doesn't clap. Finally, I turn around, panting heavily with the exertion, and peer out into the auditorium. It takes a few moments for it to sink in but, like a punch into my stomach, I see half the seats are empty. I don't understand. A rage descends over me. Throwing my baton down, I storm off the stage and into the side wings where I see the stage manager and my agent. 'What was that about?' I yell at them. 'I thought we'd sold out.'

'We didn't want to tell you, but the box office told us they'd been inundated with people demanding their money back.'

'What on earth for? Why?'

'We don't know exactly… some sort of boycott, we think.'

'A what?' I know I am screaming but I can't help it.

'We think it's to do with your appearance in court.'

I put my face in my hands and scream. I storm to my dressing room and, slamming the door shut behind me, pace up and down unable to believe that it had come to this. I pour myself a whisky and gulp it down in one. I stand there with the empty glass in my hand, shaking from head to foot while my throat burns. I catch my reflection in the mirror – a man in a tuxedo, bow tie undone, his face red with anger and sweat, a man contaminated, and for the first time in my life I hate what I see. I fling the glass at the mirror, shattering it.

Half an hour later, having ordered another glass and drunk too much whisky, there was a knock on the door. 'Leave me alone,' I shouted.

'Maestro, sir,' came the nervous voice from the other side. 'There's someone to see you.'

'Tell them to–'

'They say they've got something of yours and that it is important.'

I hesitated but of course who can resist something like that. I staggered to my feet, feeling distinctly woozy, and

117

opened the door.

'Good evening, Maestro,' he said, walking straight past me to stand in the middle of my dressing room. He took in the mirror but said nothing.

'Jesus, what are you doing here?'

'I've come to give you this back,' he said, holding something curled up in his hand.

'What is it?'

He opened his palm and let something unfurl from his fingers. 'It's your tie.'

'Yes,' I said, transfixed by its many colours.

'Isabelle wanted you to have it back. She said you weren't to try and contact her again. Also, she asked me to give you another message.'

I looked at him expectantly. 'Yes? What is it?'

'It's this.'

Hell, the pain. It felt like a sledgehammer had slammed into my face. I fell back, falling against my chair and landing awkwardly amidst the shards of broken glass. My whole face felt as if it had ballooned, pulsating with pain. My vision blurred, blood poured from my nose and from a cut in my hand where I'd landed on the broken glass. Jacques transformed himself into two before throwing the tie at me, spinning on his heels, and leaving.

Annecy, March 1969

I knew my career would be in tatters but I hadn't expected it to be torn apart quite so spectacularly. On the Monday morning following the disastrous Saturday concert, my record bosses telephoned me to tell me they were due to have discussions about my future. I could expect to hear from them the following week. That same day I went to see my doctor about my broken nose. Meanwhile, on Wednesday, after two days of deliberations, the jury returned their verdict on Hilda Lapointe. Unsurprisingly, they found her guilty of war crimes. The next week, my record label called me in for a meeting. Having asked what had happened to my nose, they told me that through my association with a war criminal, I had become a liability both to myself and, more importantly, to the label. They had no option but to release me. When I hinted at compensation, they told me I was lucky they had decided against suing me. Apparently, there was a standard clause in my contract about not bringing the label into ill-repute. Two days later, Hilda was back in court to hear the sentence – she got five years. The papers led the public outcry, saying it was far too lenient. They reckoned she'd be out within three years. It was a national disgrace, they said, a slap in the face for those who had suffered during the war.

I received no word from Isabelle. Not that I had expected to. I missed her terribly and spent weeks pining for her.

Things got worse. If I thought my royalties would keep me afloat, again I was to be disappointed. My record sales dried up entirely. I had no work and no income.

The case, and the sentence, also upset Michèle, bringing back too many painful memories of the war. Her indifference towards me deepened, first to resentment then anger. How could I have spoken up for her, she kept asking, how could I have done it. I had no answer; I didn't truly know myself. I wanted to use words like 'honour' and 'debt', but they sounded too hollow, too inadequate.

Come Christmas 1968, Michèle announced she was leaving me. I'd been half expecting it. I thought I'd be devastated but, in the end, it came almost as a relief. She'd been seeing someone else, she said, a dentist, someone she was very much in love with and someone she wanted to marry. Of course, I thought, the wonderful dentist. I wondered how he'd managed to bring out her love when I, after so many years, had failed.

Oddly enough, we got on better in those last few weeks than we had for years, with the exception of our holiday in Morocco. It was probably the relief. We reached an amicable settlement, sold the house and split the proceeds. With my share, I bought a modest little house with a small garden in a tiny village outside the town of Annecy, near the Swiss border, about 40 kilometres south of Geneva. With its low ceilings and stone floors and old-fashioned wooden furniture, the house is what one might describe as rustic; a far cry from Paris. Here, in this village, stuck sometime in the previous century, no one recognised me. I was yesterday's news and already forgotten. Also, my longer hair and newly-shaped nose acted as a disguise. I bought a puppy, a short-legged Jack Russell, and called him Claude – after Claude Debussy. In March, I found a job in a warehouse in town, and tried my best to adapt to my new circumstances.

The town of Annecy lies on a lake and on Sundays, Claude and I would walk round its perimeter, admiring the views, soothed by its calm waters. In the evenings, with Claude nestled on my lap, I'd watch television, read the papers or the monthly classical music magazine, *Diapason*, and go to bed to dream of Isabelle.

But it was Hilda that occupied my thoughts.

Rennes, October 1969

In April 1969, Charles de Gaulle resigned as president. Elections for his successor took place in June. I went to the polling station in Annecy to cast my vote. I handed over my identification to the old woman working there. Having found my name on her list, she looked up quizzically at me and asked, 'Aren't you–'

'No,' I snapped. 'We just share the same name.'

'You look like him.'

'No, I'm far more handsome.'

I voted for Georges Pompidou for no other reason than I liked his name. He duly won and became our new president.

Every day I thought less of Isabelle and more of Hilda. I constantly wondered how she was getting on. She'd been incarcerated at the *Centre Pénitentiaire de Rennes*, a women's prison in Brittany. I hoped she was suffering. I hated her for what she'd done to me, and resented the idea that she'd taken the credit for supposedly having saved me but none of the flak for having, in effect, destroyed me. I was determined she should know, that she should apologise for having caused all my misfortune. Some nights, unable to sleep, I relived Madame Kahn's testimony, visualising those poor women naked on the ice while she whipped them across the breasts. Sometimes, I fantasised about killing her. I would buy poison, I decided, strychnine perhaps, and administer it to her via a homemade cake. After all, they say Alexander the Great was killed by the stuff. But I am no murderer. Yet, the thought of seeing her began to obsess me. I wanted to see her in prison, miserable, repentant for all the things she had done.

Unable to bear it any more, I wrote a letter to the prison authorities in Rennes, expressing the desire to visit my "old friend", and, having posted it off, waited for the reply. It came two weeks later. Yes, it said, Hilda Lapointe would see me. I was given a specific date and time.

And so, at the crack of dawn on a bright but chilly autumn day in October 1969, I embarked on the seven-hour train journey to Rennes, changing at Montparnasse in Paris. It was the first time I'd been in the capital since my departure a few months before but I had no desire to see it, and remained in the station platform's waiting room until I was able to board the train to Rennes. The return train fare was not cheap. This, in itself, was a new sensation – I'd never had to worry about money before, I just had it. Now, things were different – I was having to budget and mind the centimes.

I settled down on the train, and, eating my cheese baguette, began to read the latest edition of *Diapason*. I may have been shunned but I was still interested in reading about the world of classical music. I knew, from the previous edition, that the Americans had found a replacement for me in whom they had high hopes. On the day of his first performance, I even sent him a telegram wishing him luck. I tried to mean it but, in truth, I rather hoped to see him fail. The magazine helped pass time on the train. But then, having reached page thirteen, my mouth hung open, my mind whirling – there, looking stunning, was a photograph of Isabelle. My heart thumped as I read the accompanying interview, barely able to take in the words. I'd absorbed enough to see that she been taken on by my old label as a soloist and was due to record her first record soon. *Gifted with a natural talent,* concluded the article, *Isabelle has a bright future in front of her. And she'll enjoy the support of her new husband and manager, Jacques. We wish them both well.* I threw the magazine to one side and felt myself overwhelmed with a sense of longing and regret.

Rennes, at a cursory glance, seemed an attractive town. But ignoring it, and with no time or desire to explore, I caught a taxi straight to the prison. There, I had my bag searched, my magazine flipped through, and went through all the other security checks. Satisfied, the guard then took me to a bare, grey-bricked, airless room and told me to wait. I took a plastic seat and sat with my hands on my lap, watching as various people and prison staff came and went. Only now did I begin to regret my haste. Yet, I knew, having come this far, I had to go through with it. I felt as if I couldn't get on with my new life until I had confronted her and finally put the whole sorry episode behind me. I had wanted an apology but I knew that was expecting too much. I wanted something from her, I just couldn't work out what it was. Perhaps if I had stayed in court that day, I would have heard what I needed to hear.

Half an hour later, I was called through. My heart skipped a beat on hearing my name. I followed the female guard across a courtyard, up a flight of steps, and through a maze of corridors, stopping behind her as she unlocked and relocked numerous doors and gates. The guard escorted me into a large room full of tables and chairs, some already occupied by fellow visitors, and told me to take a seat. Was this it? I wondered. I rather expected a partition between us and them, but no, we were to share a table as if enjoying a coffee in a café, albeit a bleak one.

A door opened at the far end of the hall, and in came two guards followed by a number of prisoners, each wearing handcuffs, and all dressed identically in grey prison overalls. There were waves and embraces. I searched for Hilda and found her, last in the queue. On seeing me, she nodded and strode towards me. She sat on the opposite side of the table from me, leaning back on the chair, fixing me with a steely stare.

'Hello, Hilda. How are you?' Stupid question, I thought.

'I'm fine, as you can see.' She had managed, somehow, to have gained weight, although it might have been illusion in the shapeless overalls. But her shoulders looked square, her jaw likewise. She had the pallor of someone lacking sunlight on her skin, her face was almost grey, her eyes deep-set.

'Why do you want to see me?' she asked, bypassing all small talk.

'I don't know,' I stuttered. 'I suppose I wanted to see how you were.'

'I'm fine – I told you and, as you can see, I am here, and I am well, all things considered.'

'Are you... are you treated well?'

She pulled a face which I interpreted as a reluctant yes. 'What happened to your nose?' she asked.

'I walked into a wall.'

I felt unnerved by her attitude, the unsmiling way she was looking at me, sitting there with the handcuffs round her

126

wrists. 'Do you get any other visitors?'

'No, you're the first.' After a pause, she added, 'And no doubt you'll be the last.'

I'd come all this way for this?

'What you really want to know is have I repented for my sins?'

I laughed nervously. 'You make me sound like a priest.'

'They sent a priest to see me – I sent him away. What use have I for a priest? OK, as you're here, I'll tell you. I shall never say it again. Had you stayed in court and listened, you would know.' Exactly what I'd thought. 'What I said, and still say, is that I had no choice. I had to be severe, it was expected of me, and of course, I feel sorry for the women I hurt as individuals but we mustn't forget, Maestro, that they were Jews. Don't you remember what it was like before the war? Perhaps you were too young. We had that Jewish prime minister and the country was going to the dogs. Decadence, lack of morals, debauchery, corruption – that's what we had. Leftism, too much leftism. It took the Germans to bring us back into line. Of course, it's highly unfashionable to say that now, especially now that we know what we know.'

'The death camps?'

She nodded.

'But–'

'No, I may have helped the Jews onto the train but I swore in court that I didn't know what was going to happen to them. "Re-settlement" – that's all I knew. I knew not to question orders.'

'Do you regret–?'

'It's not for you to ask me that.'

We glared at each other. Eventually, I said, 'You told me once that when you saw me on that train, you thought it rare to see a youngster pursuing such noble pursuits.'

'Yes, I saw that you weren't one of *them*, a leftist, that you had a cause, a decent one. You were reading your music and I saw in you the future of France.'

'Me? Decent?' I shouted. 'Huh, I'm sorry, but you got that wrong.'

'No, I did not. You conducted beautiful music, you helped introduce the masses to what's good in life – culture, appreciation, refinement.'

'Do you really think that? You talk about the lack of morals and debauchery – that was me,' I yelled, jabbing myself in the chest. 'I may have conducted some of the finest French composers but my God, I lived a life of indulgence.'

One of the guards came over. 'Is everything OK here?' she asked.

'Yes, thank you, we're fine.' I realised that others were

looking our way. 'I'm sorry.'

She walked away slowly, keeping her eyes on us.

'You can't mean that,' whispered Hilda.

I leant towards her. 'You have no idea the amount of money I earned. Obscene amounts. And did I use my wealth to help others? Did I donate to charity; did I become a benefactor of people less fortunate than me? No, I never gave it a thought. I paid my taxes, and that was all, and even that reluctantly. I had no interest in anyone, no concern for the masses, as you call them. As long as I had my wealth, and constant admiration and gratitude, I was happy. I was unfaithful to my wife and went to bed with a beautiful younger woman. So you see, you were wrong. The young man you saved that day proved to be the very definition of what you hated. Those women you so cruelly beat had a greater sense of morality in their little fingers than I have in my whole being. You took it out on the wrong people, Hilda. It was all for nothing, everything you ever did was all for nothing.'

'No, I cannot believe this.'

'And now I've fallen from grace, cast aside, and I have nothing.'

'Oh please, now you're going to tell me that with nothing, you're happier than ever; that you lead a more fulfilling existence.' She laughed.

'No, I'm not – I'd have it back in an instant. Who wouldn't? But I would want to be younger, and be in a rock band, and take drugs, and go to orgies.'

'Do you really think I believe that? You're pathetic. Your circumstances may change but you can't change who you are.'

'You said it, Hilda, you said it.'

She leant back in her chair. 'Thank you for taking the time to visit me, Maestro.'

'Fine, I'm happy to go.'

'Good.'

I rose from my chair. The guard came over, perhaps to ensure I didn't start shouting again. I turned to leave. 'Oh, I almost forgot. I brought you a cake. Reception said it'd be OK.' I placed the box on the table, removing its lid. 'I hope you like it. It's, erm… homemade.'

*

By the time I'd returned to Annecy, it was dark and raining. From the station, I caught the bus back to my little village. All the way home from Rennes, I asked myself time and again, whether I'd been honest with Hilda – would I want it all again? Perhaps, I thought, perhaps. All I did know was that, having seen her, I would never see her again.

Exhausted after such a long day, I opened the door to my

house and was greeted by an over-excited and hungry Claude. I let him out for a pee and then fed him. Having dried him off, I put on some Moroccan music and settled down for the evening with Claude on his back on my lap, and felt a surge of affection for my little home. As I tapped my foot and tickled Claude's stomach, I realised it had taken the whole day but Hilda had given me the answer I was looking for after all – I had no desire to go back to my old life.

Part Three

Annecy, September 1982

'I think perhaps, after all, I will have that cup of tea.' *M Bowen*

'And why not, Monsieur Bowen, why not.'

I left him sitting in my squashy settee, reading his notes. 'So, you weren't tempted to get another dog?'

'Yes,' I shouted from the kitchen as I poured water into the kettle. 'But it's too soon. Claude only died earlier this year. He was fourteen, poor old thing.'

I made the tea and found a packet of biscuits and arranged a few on a plate.

'Sugar?'

'No thanks.' I handed him his tea and the plate. 'Thank you. You never re-married then, Maestro?'

'No. I'm still waiting for Isabelle.'

'Are you?'

I laughed. 'No, sadly not. I never heard from her again but I know she's still doing well.'

135

'Still married to that Jesus fellow?'

'Jacques. No. I heard they'd divorced. Recently. That came as a surprise.'

'You seem to know a lot about her,' he said, tackling a biscuit.

'I look out for her, and she's often mentioned in that music magazine.'

'Yes, she's considered the country's top cellist.'

'Indeed. Here's to Isabelle and her continued success,' I said, raising my cup of tea.

'And you, Maestro – you've never been tempted to return to music?'

'No, not now. I'm too old now anyway.'

'Nonsense, you're only what – sixty?'

'Sixty, going on eighty.'

'But, of course, what I really want to know, is what happened to Hilda Lapointe. We know you didn't actually poison her!'

'No! Tempting as it was.'

'And that she was released in 1971–'

'Yes, she'd served three years.'

'But after that, whoosh – she just vanished.' He took a sip of his tea. 'I asked the prison whether they knew where she was but they didn't know, or, more likely, they didn't want to tell me. Do you know, Maestro?'

'Me? No. I never did go see her again. She probably changed her name again. She'd be 82 now.'

'If she's still alive.'

'Exactly.'

He glanced at his watch. 'Well, Maestro, I've taken enough of your time and I've got a long way to go.' He slipped his pen into his inside pocket and put his notepad into his briefcase. 'I know you have to pop out soon.'

'What?'

'You said you have to go and see a neighbour, or something.'

'Oh, yes, of course. I ought to go and do my duty.'

'Very good of you.' He struggled out of the settee. Pulling the creases out of his jacket, he offered me his hand. 'It's been a real pleasure.'

'The pleasure's all mine, Monsieur Bowen. Now, have you got everything? Good. I'll see you out.'

'Thank you.'

'I think it might rain soon,' I said, stepping outside with him. 'When do you think the article will appear?'

'After the photographer's been over. I'll get her to give you a ring. Then probably a week or so after that.'

'That's fine. I look forward to reading about myself,' I

said, aware that I'd let slip a hint of my old vanity.

'Yes, well. Thank you for the tea.'

'Have a good trip back.'

'I will. Thank you. Goodbye, Maestro.'

'Goodbye, Monsieur Bowen. Goodbye.' I watched him leave, in his dapper cream-coloured suit, and thought, what a charming fellow.

*

Returning indoors, I ate another biscuit and finished my tea. Yes, I thought, I'd better go – it was almost three. She doesn't like it if I'm late. Not that she ever goes anywhere, but she likes the routine.

I felt strangely content – as if I'd just purged myself of something unpleasant. I felt lighter somehow. Is this how Catholics feel after confession, I wondered. Donning my overcoat and taking my umbrella, I closed my front door behind me, and made my way down the road. I told Monsieur Bowen I was visiting a neighbour but in fact, they lived right at the far end of the village. I strode across the village square and past the church, and along another street lined with picturesque cottages and well-tended gardens, a spring in my step, waving to various people whom I knew by sight. I was wrong about the rain – indeed, the sun was appearing from the clouds. I stopped by at the village shop and brought a newspaper, a dozen eggs, powdered milk and a small assortment of vegetables. What a fine day it'd been. I thoroughly enjoyed unburdening myself. And what a pleasant young man was Monsieur Bowen, Henri. I was sure he would do the article justice. And here it is, the house. I pushed open the gate and admired the front garden which I had, just a few days previously, spent some time clearing and weeding, dead-heading the plants and flowers. Having my own key, I let myself in.

'Only me,' I shouted as I closed the door behind me.

'I'm in here,' she shouted back from the living room. Not that she'd be anywhere else.

'I got you your paper and the groceries you asked for.' I said, handing her the newspaper. She spent the whole day in her living room, sitting in an old armchair with a blanket over her knees, a small space cluttered with too much furniture and too many paintings on the wall, and a mantelpiece adorned with cheap horse figurines. In the corner, opposite her, the television was on, the volume turned down. Next to her, on a high, small table, a blue-coloured budgerigar in its cage. 'How's Pompidou?' I asked.

'A bit quiet today, aren't you, Pompy? Next time you pass the shop, can you get me some more birdseed?'

'Sure.'

'And some more headache pills.'

'Again?'

She glanced at the paper's headlines. 'I don't know why I read the paper,' she said. 'It's nothing but bad news.'

Stepping into her tiny kitchen, I packed away the groceries. Returning, I asked her how she was.

'I feel very stiff today.'

'Well, I keep telling you, Hilda, you ought to get up and about. Walk up to the square and back. It'd do you the world of good.'

'I know, I know,' she said, readjusting her blanket.

'Are you warm enough? Can I make you a cup of tea?'

'Maestro, I'm fine. Will you stop fussing?'

'Well, you know, I like to make sure you're OK. None of us are getting any younger.'

She attempted a smile. 'You're so kind. I don't know how I would cope without you.' The words were appreciative, and she said them occasionally, but I always felt as if she was saying them for the sake of it; because she felt she had to; it never felt as if it came from the heart.

'Ah, it's nothing,' I said, playing my part.

'It's been many years now, hasn't it?'

'Yes, I suppose it has. But someone had to look after you,

eh?'

'Did you say something about a cup of tea?'

I laughed. 'Coming right up, Hilda, coming right up.'

Annecy, October 1982

A couple days after Monsieur Bowen's visit, came the photographer. A young woman in a hurry. She declined my offer of a drink and kept her mackintosh on, its belt flapping behind her. She did her business quickly and efficiently, thanked me and left. I was rather disappointed how little time it took.

Each day, I bought Hilda her paper and quickly flicked through its pages to see whether my interview had appeared yet. I did wonder what she'd make of it. I feared she'd be cross but she knew what I was like, and, heck, I thought, the world had given her up for dead; it had no interest in her any more.

I hadn't been quite honest with Monsieur Bowen. I did visit Hilda in prison again. A week or so after my first visit, I received a short letter from her. It merely thanked me for the cake, saying how delicious it was. I was so pleasantly surprised that, a few weeks later, I made another and set off all the way to Rennes to deliver it to her. And that's how it started.

Despite the distance and the effort, not to mention the cost, I went once a month for the rest of her sentence. I didn't like leaving Claude by himself for so long a day, but, as I told him, it wasn't often.

Once there, we talked about the news, the gossip and even, to my surprise, sport. She read the papers everyday, devouring what was going on in France and around the world. She was fascinated by the on-going war in Vietnam; she adored the cyclist, Eddie Merckx, who had won the Tour de France that year, and liked to pour scorn on Georges Pompidou and the work of his government.

Towards the end of her sentence, I brought up the subject of where she was going to live following her release. Although she still had her apartment in Paris, she was determined never to return to the capital. I knew the feeling. I helped her sell the flat and, with the proceeds, bought a little cottage in the same village as mine near Annecy. In October 1971, after exactly three years in prison, Hilda was released. I met her at the prison gates, and took her to Annecy and her new home, fearful of what she'd think of it. She liked it. Almost immediately, however, she became a recluse, rarely venturing out, content to sit at home all day, or sitting out in the small garden at the back, reading the papers. I suggested she buy a pet and took Claude round to visit. She wasn't the slightest bit interested in the dog and asked me never to bring 'that mongrel' round again. But she did buy a budgerigar – the first of many.

Eleven years later, little had changed but now, aged 82, she suffers from her age.

*

Ten days after the photographer's visit, it was there! My interview. I was already half way from the shop to Hilda's cottage, when I saw it. *Whatever happened to the Maestro?* said the headline. *Once, he was renowned and feted throughout France as the future of classical music. Yet, just when his star was at its zenith, just when it seemed he could do no wrong, the Maestro, as he was commonly known, stood by a former guard from the wartime concentration camp at Drancy. It proved a fateful mistake and left him with his career in tatters, forcing him to disappear. Now, 14 years on, we've tracked him down and sent our top music reporter, Henri Bowen, to see him. After so many years of silence, the Maestro finally has his say…*

I didn't like the photo, though. I hadn't realised how old I looked. But here, in this black and white photo, I looked thin and drawn and grey. Nonetheless, excited, I rushed over to Hilda's, deciding to buy myself a copy on the way back.

I didn't stay too long at Hilda's, just long enough to give her the newspaper and make sure she was all right. I didn't mention the interview – she'd find it soon enough.

I returned to the shop and to my utter disappointment, found they'd sold out of the newspaper. Not to worry, I thought, I'd read Hilda's copy the following day.

*

First thing the following morning, I rang her to ask if I could come and visit her straightaway. Having delayed it a day, I couldn't wait to read the interview. To my surprise, she didn't answer. Perhaps it's bath day, I thought. I decided not to wait – I'd simply walk over now.

I let myself in. 'Only me,' I shouted. 'Hope you don't mind, but I've come early. I have to pop out later, so I thought I'd come see you now instead.' No answer. 'Hello? Hilda?'

It was past nine o'clock – she wouldn't still be in bed. No, she'd been up – I noticed her post propped up on the mantelpiece. Surely, she hadn't gone out. Hilda never went out unless necessity forced her into it. It was now that I felt the first real pangs of concern. 'Hilda?' I shouted again.

She was nowhere downstairs, nor in the garden. Coming back indoors, I ran up the stairs, knocked on her bedroom door, and, having received no reply, opened it. She wasn't there. Her bed was made, everything was as it was supposed to be.

From there, I tried the bathroom door. It was locked. I tapped gently on the door and again called out her name. Still no response. I knocked harder, then harder still, shouting her name, to the point I was thumping on the door, rattling the doorknob. I'd become frantic. I had no choice – I had to break down the door. Bracing myself, I barged against the door with my shoulder. It didn't budge. There was no way I was going to force it open by jumping against it. Having an idea, I ran downstairs and back into her garden and to her shed, where I knew I'd find an axe.

I suffered a moment's hesitation at the thought of ruining a perfectly good bathroom door. 'Hilda, are you there? Are you OK?' Silence. 'For heaven's sake, answer me.' I swung the axe, splintering the wood. Again and again, I hacked at it, getting faster all the time, my breaths coming in panicked bursts. Eventually I'd made enough of a split to be able to see. Peering through the gap, I could see her – in her bath, the head thrown back, an arm dangling over the side. She was wearing her clothes. 'Hilda, what have you done?' I slashed further at the door until, finally, I was able to squeeze my arm through and, after a bit of fumbling, managed to unlock the bolt. I almost fell in, slipping on the fragments of wood on the bathroom tiles.

'Hilda?' I held my breath. She had had a bath fully

dressed. The water, up to her neck, was coloured red.

Annecy, November 1982

Aged 82, Hilda Lapointe, *née* Irène d'Urville, had committed suicide. Somehow, the papers had picked up on it and published the story. They reckoned that, finally, after almost forty years, her guilt had caught up with her. They were utterly wrong. She'd never felt guilt.

The post I thought I saw that morning, propped up on her mantelpiece, was in fact one single envelope – addressed to me. A policewoman brought it round to mine later that day. Using a letter opener, I sliced it open and, in front of the policewoman, nervously unfolded the single sheet of paper. The note contained just five words. It read: *Don't forget to feed Pompidou.* 'You bitch,' I screamed.

Shocked, the policewoman asked if I was OK.

I apologised and groaned – for I knew she'd tell her colleagues that I'd sworn and what an unfeeling, nasty man I was.

148

Over the days that followed, I arranged a funeral for her. She had enough money in her account to cover it all. There was to be a delay, however. The local coroner had ordered an autopsy. I think they wanted to ensure that she had really taken her own life and that I hadn't killed her off. I remembered her lawyer all those years ago telling me she once talked of suicide.

What little money was left over, including the house and its contents, was, according to her will, to be passed to a nephew of the woman she used to know in Saint-Romain after the war. Someone who, as far as I knew, had never visited her, never wrote, not even a Christmas card. I was disappointed but not surprised; I hadn't expected it to come my way. There wasn't much of it anyway. I knew full well that she'd been using me these last eleven years. I'd become her cleaner, her shopper, her cook, her gardener, her unpaid skivvy. She'd never once, in all that time, thanked me. The occasional, insincere word of appreciation, perhaps, but never a 'thank you'.

The autopsy returned a verdict of suicide by the cutting of the wrists and an overdose of headache tablets. So, that was why she kept making me buy them. She'd planned it, slowly hoarding the pills. Why had she done it? I wasn't sure but it wasn't guilt. But I do know that my interview in the newspaper had tipped her over the edge. That was my intention, perhaps not to kill herself, but to hurt her, to make her see that still after all these years, people would remember her for what she was — a cruel, sadistic woman who never expressed any remorse for the dreadful things she did. And through the interview, I'd ensured that people would *remember*.

I felt no pity yet, in a strange way, I rather missed her. I missed the routine of going round to see her day after day.

*

Hilda's funeral took place on a cold and breezy but sunny November morning, the clouds moving briskly across the sky, the late autumnal colours a joy to behold, the graveyard awash with a carpet of orange-brown leaves. Hilda had never shown the slightest interest in the church. Still, we have to do these things. There were just the three of us — me, the priest and, to my surprise, the nephew, Gérard, a tall, slim man in his fifties with a pointed chin, sporting a watch chain across his waistcoat. I think he, at least, had been driven by guilt. Before the service began, he apologised for never having visited. I gave him Hilda's keys and told him to deal with the house as he saw fit. We shook hands and stood next to each other as the priest did his bit.

We therefore commit Hilda's body to the ground; earth to earth, ashes to ashes, dust to dust…

Afterwards, the three of us stood with our hands clasped in front of us, and looked down at Hilda's coffin inside its grave. I thought of Madame Kahn, and the poor woman Hilda had beaten to death on the ice; I thought of her sitting impassively in court, her eyes cold while those around her wept; I thought of me as a young man on that train. Was that really *me*? It seemed such a long time ago, so long it felt as if the memory belonged to someone else. We may have been at war but, looking back, I envied that young man with his hopes and ambition. He knew exactly what he wanted from life, knew exactly where he was going. But I was a lonely young boy, I knew that. Marriage, success, fame and wealth – and all the time I remained lonely. And now, so many years on, with Hilda gone, I was lonely once more.

The church clock struck twelve. As the last peal faded away, the priest asked to be excused. Gérard and I watched as he scuttled off towards the church, his cassock caught by the breeze, exposing a pair of trainers. I spied an elderly gentleman waiting at the church entrance, leaning against his shovel.

'Well, that's it,' said Gérard.

'Yes.' I sighed. 'That's truly it.'

'Have you noticed something?' he said, his eyes still fixed on the coffin.

I shook my head.

'Don't make it obvious, but the whole time we've been here, there's been someone watching us, standing next to the elm tree behind us.'

I hadn't noticed. Slowly, the two of us turned round. Gérard was right – there was someone, a woman dressed in funereal black, right down to a veil over her face.

'Is it someone you know?' he asked.

'Yes,' I said, squinting my eyes against the autumn sun. 'I think it is. You'll have to excuse me.'

Slowly, I walked towards her, my hands behind my back, my shoes crunching the dried leaves underfoot. I watched her as she stepped away from the long shadow of the tree. Lifting her veil, she said quietly, 'Hello, Maestro.'

I smiled. 'Isabelle. I'd hoped you'd come. How lovely to see you again.'

THE END

Novels by Rupert Colley:

The Love and War Series

The Woman on the Train

The White Venus

The Black Maria

My Brother the Enemy

Anastasia

The Searight Saga

This Time Tomorrow

The Unforgiving Sea

The Red Oak

Rupertcolley.com

To obtain Rupert's moving short story, *Elena*, and join his Mailing List and be the first to know of future releases, etc, please go to:
http://eepurl.com/9-M2H

Party because
he was
she was lonely
or did he think she
would repent or thank him.